Springtime
for
Murder

Debbie Young

Copyright Information

SPRINGTIME FOR MURDER
by Debbie Young

© Debbie Young 2018
Published by Hawkesbury Press 2018
Hawkesbury Upton, Gloucestershire, England
Cover design by Rachel Lawston of Lawston Design
Illustration of Hector's House © T E Shepherd 2018

ISBN (paperback) 978 1 911 223 344
ISBN (ebook) 978 1 911 223 337

About the Author

Debbie Young writes warm, witty, feel-good fiction.

Her Sophie Sayers Village Mystery series of seven novels runs the course of a year in the fictional Cotswold village of Wendlebury Barrow. Her Staffroom at St Bride's series set in a girls' boarding school in the same parish runs from the start of an academic year. Her Tales from Wendlebury Barrow Quick Reads series features Sophie and friends, as well as introducing new local characters.

Debbie's humorous short stories are available in themed collections, such as *Marry in Haste*, *Quick Change* and *Stocking Fillers*, and in many anthologies.

She is a frequent speaker at literature festivals and writers' events and is founder and director of the free Hawkesbury Upton Literature Festival.

A regular contributor to two local community magazines, the award-winning *Tetbury Advertiser* and the *Hawkesbury Parish News*, she has published two collections of her columns, *Young by Name* and *All Part of the Charm*. These publications offer insight into her own life in a small Cotswold village where she lives with her Scottish husband and their teenage daughter.

For the latest information about Debbie's
books and events, visit her Writing Life website,
where you may also like to join her free Readers' Club:
www.authordebbieyoung.com

Also by Debbie Young

Sophie Sayers Village Mysteries
Best Murder in Show (1)
Trick or Murder? (2)
Murder in the Manger (3)
Murder by the Book (4)
Murder Your Darlings (6)
Murder Lost and Found (7) – coming 2021

Staffroom at St Bride's School Mysteries
Secrets at St Bride's (1)
Stranger at St Bride's (2)
Scandal at St Bride's (3) – coming 2021

Tales from Wendlebury Barrow (Quick Reads)
The Natter of Knitters
The Clutch of Eggs

Short Story Collections
Marry in Haste
Quick Change
Stocking Fillers

Essay Collections
All Part of the Charm:
*   A Modern Memoir of English Village Life*
Young By Name:
*   Whimsical Columns from the Tetbury Advertiser*

To my brother and sister

"The grave's a fine and private place,
But none, I think, do there embrace."

Andrew Marvell

"Being neighbourly isn't a question of
how long you've lived somewhere.
It's a matter of human kindness.
You don't need to have Wendlebury Barrow
on your birth certificate
to pick up its spirit."

Sophie Sayers

Springtime
for
Murder

Debbie Young

HAWKESBURY
— PRESS —

1 Funny Bunny

Sina slammed her skipping rope down on the trade counter to get Hector's attention. "My brother and me have just found the Easter Bunny lying dead in a grave in the churchyard."

Hector looked up from his spreadsheet. "Are you sure, Sina?"

"Yes, and Tommy said to fetch you to sort it out."

"I'm afraid dealing with mythical beasts isn't in the bookseller's job description." Hector glanced at his watch. "Besides, I can't leave the bookshop till the Battersby rep has been, and she's due any minute now. But don't worry, Sophie will come with you to have a look, won't you, Sophie?"

I set down a tray of crockery on the tearoom counter so abruptly that a cup broke. "And since when has it been part of my job description? You're meant to be on my side."

As my boyfriend as well as my boss, Hector knew I didn't like visiting the churchyard.

"The Easter Bunny?" asked old Billy, pouring an extravagant amount of cream into his teacup. "He's early. Easter's weeks away."

I was glad about that. On Palm Sunday, I was due to start running the village Sunday School class. I still didn't know how I'd let the vicar talk me into volunteering.

Billy licked a drip off the cream jug's spout. "What's the Easter Bunny doing in my grave anyway?"

Sina's eyes widened. "Your grave? How come you've got a grave when you're not even dead yet? Are you very poorly?"

She went to perch on the chair beside his and laid a comforting hand on the sleeve of his ancient tweed jacket.

I was touched by her concern. "Sina, when Billy says his grave, he means he's dug it for someone else."

"But we all need graves eventually, Sina," said Billy. "Even little kiddies like you. I don't plan on meeting my maker just yet, but I shall be willing enough when the good Lord decides it's my time."

Sina frowned. "Who will dig your grave, Billy?"

Billy wiped his hands on his trousers.

"Your brother, I expect. I've been training him."

"Is that like work experience?" asked Sina.

More like work avoidance for Billy. He often gets Tommy to do his dirty work in return for pocket money or some dubious favour. Tommy would be an industrious digger, with the enthusiasm of a Labrador puppy and about as much accuracy. But I kept that thought to myself. I didn't want to deter Billy from accompanying us to the churchyard. Besides, the graves were his responsibility, not mine.

Hector chuckled. "An internship on interment. No doubt Tommy's hoping to find buried treasure."

Billy's mouth twitched. "I'm not saying I didn't put that idea in his head to get him interested in helping me. But by rights, gravedigging is a two-man job: one to dig,

2

the other to make sure the sides don't collapse on top of him. Of course, you shore up the sides with wooden boards as you go, but it's still a risky business if you don't do it right. A couple of tons of earth falling too fast for you to climb up your little ladder, and within minutes you'd be stone dead."

I'd never seen a grave with a ladder in it. Sina asked exactly what I was thinking.

"What's the ladder for? In case the person you've buried isn't quite dead?"

Billy shook his head. "Quite the opposite. It's for the gravedigger's benefit. You must always leave a ladder at the end until you're done digging. Them's the rules. Health and safety, even in death."

"I hadn't realised digging graves was such a complicated business," I said.

"It's ain't a business," said Billy. "It's a craft. I'd better come along with you for safety's sake."

He got up, buttoned his ancient tweed jacket and headed for the door, Sina prancing after him like Puck after Bottom.

When Hector got up from his stool to join me behind the tearoom counter, I thought he'd come to show solidarity. Instead, he put his arm round my shoulders and guided me firmly out into the street.

"Go on, sweetheart, the fresh air will do you good."

Like a curly-haired sheepdog directing a reluctant ewe, he blocked the shop doorway behind me. There was no escape.

As I caught up with the advance investigation party, Sina slipped her hand into mine, reminding me how young she was. I wanted to reassure her, despite my own nerves.

3

"It's probably just an old scarecrow that someone's put there as a practical joke. Are you sure it's not just your brother winding you up?"

Zigzagging beside me, Sina took twice as many paces as I did.

"If he is, I'll push him in the grave on top of it and fill it in."

I was glad her usual spirit was returning. Being Tommy's little sister would be enough to make any girl resilient.

Billy scowled. "My churchyard ain't no playpark. It's sacred ground, consecrated for burials, not for kiddies to lark about in. Like the poet says, 'The grave's a fine and private place, but none, I think, do there embrace.'"

I had no idea where that came from. Billy grinned at my puzzled expression.

"You and your clever-clogs boyfriend ain't the only ones who can quote poetry."

Actually, only Hector could, but I wasn't about to put myself down.

"I recites poems about graveyards while I'm digging, to set a good rhythm." He repeated his quote, punctuating it with a mime. 'The grave's *(dig)* a fine *(throw)* and private *(dig)* place *(throw)*.'" He stopped shovelling to tap his forehead. "Grey's *Elegy* is another good 'un." Stretching his arms out towards the mid-morning sun, he began to declaim, "'The curfew tolls the knell of parting day—'"

"Does Tommy use the same method when he's digging?" He might have been gaining more than muscles from his labours.

"I don't think my brother knows any poetry," said Sina. "Unless you count limericks. He knows loads of them."

4

I bet Billy did too, but not the type suitable for young ears, so I tried to move the conversation on.

"I don't think a graveyard is the right place for limericks. It should be a serious place."

"Not necessarily, girlie," said Billy. "You'd be surprised. I has long chats sometimes with them that comes to visit their loved ones there, and we often have a laugh thinking about times gone by."

"Isn't that a bit disrespectful?"

Billy gave me a reproachful look. "You've got this all wrong, you know. Graveyards are places full of memories, and who wouldn't rather remember the fun times?" He looked away from me, his voice tightening with emotion. "A churchyard is a landscape full of love."

I turned to Sina to allow him to recover his composure.

"Anyway, never mind about poetry, I'm sure Billy and I will help you get to the bottom of this Easter Bunny mystery in no time."

She stopped jigging about and fixed me with a wide-eyed stare. "But I don't want to get to the bottom of it. I'm not getting down into a smelly old grave, even if you are."

"I don't mean we will literally get into the grave, Sina, just that we'll find out what's going on and put an end to it."

"Besides, graves smell lovely," said Billy. "The most natural scent in the world – freshly dug soil."

As we crossed the road to St Bride's, I tugged at her hand, as if coaxing a stubborn puppy on a leash, and she carried on dancing about at my side. Fumbling to open the lychgate, I tried not to let Sina see my hands shaking.

Tommy's gangly teenage frame was pressed up against the boundary wall, which in the morning sunshine was the colour of local honey. He pointed towards a large rectangular hole in the grass a few metres in front of him. A sheet of artificial turf big enough to cover the hole lay crumpled on the ground beside it. The real grass, dotted with early daisies, was still glossy with dew, the spring sunshine not yet hot enough to burn it off. So many dead people beneath our feet pushing those daisies up, I thought with a shudder.

Tommy, usually fearless, spoke in a low voice, as if worried about being overheard. "The body's in there, miss."

Sina, gripping my hand even tighter, crept towards the open grave with commendable stealth. I had no option but to advance beside her. Billy followed.

Together we stopped at the edge of the open grave. Below the perfectly incised turf, dense, rich soil the colour of coffee grounds – or of dried blood – was shored up by wooden boards. The hole, much deeper than I'd expected, exuded a pure, rich smell of wet earth. Towards the bottom, the colour and texture of the soil changed, becoming drier and stonier, reminding me of cross-section diagrams in geology books. At one end stood a narrow ladder.

At the bottom of the grave, as still as a house brick, lay the body of a very old lady, about five feet long and clothed in an old-fashioned mink coat. One sugar-pink velour carpet slipper protruded beneath the hem. I could see how Sina and Tommy had mistaken it at a quick glance for the sole of a not-so-lucky rabbit's foot. A giant rabbit's foot, that is.

But most striking of all was the pair of fake rabbit ears, in a blue floral sprigged cotton, that added twenty centimetres to the body's height. I recognised the style of the ears from the Easter display in the village shop. Its proprietor Carol Barker sold home-made seasonal dressing-up clothes to boost her precarious takings. Currently, dozens of pairs of bunny ears were tempting small children from a basket on the shop counter.

She lay with her hands raised beside her head, her body slightly twisted to one side, her left knee bent more than the right. My hand itched for a piece of chalk to draw around her, because she formed the typical shape of a dead body outlined on the ground in police crime scene investigations.

The body lay too neatly on the ground for her to have fallen down the hole, but I couldn't imagine anyone climbing down the ladder and lying down of their own accord. She looked as if someone must have carried her down and laid her out as if on a mortuary slab.

Billy, swaying gently beside me, put his hand on my shoulder to steady himself. "That's no Easter Bunny," he said, his voice cracking. "That's my Auntie Bunny. Bunny Carter. My mother's late brother was her first husband."

"Oh my goodness, Billy, I'm so sorry—" I began, but he cut me off.

"So what's the silly old fool playing at now?"

2 Down the Rabbit Hole

"Billy!" cried Tommy, still rigid against the wall. "You're always telling me to be more respectful in the churchyard. How come it's all right for you to slag off dead people?"

Billy crossed to the wall to pick up the long-handled scythe he used for clearing churchyard weeds. "What makes you think she's dead?"

Tommy steeled himself to leave his post and peer over the edge of the grave. "She doesn't look exactly lively."

"Old ladies don't usually move about much," said Sina.

"My Auntie Bunny certainly doesn't." Billy turned the scythe upside down and grasped the blade. "She's hardly left her house for years." I flinched, fearing for the flesh of palm. He lowered the handle of the scythe into the grave and gave the old lady a vigorous prod. A faint, low moan drifted up to reassure us that she was still alive.

"There, told you so," said Billy, retrieving the scythe and spinning it round to grasp the handle. "It would take a lot more than a tumble down a hole to kill this old bird. She ain't ready to go yet."

The children brightened at the news.

"Do you want me to go down and help her back up?" asked Tommy. He did so love to help. "I like going up and down that little ladder. I could try out my new fireman's lift that I've been practising on Sina."

"NO!" Sina and I said at once.

"We shouldn't move her till a paramedic's checked her out," I continued. "Moving her at this stage could do more harm than good. Besides we shouldn't be disturbing the ground around her. It might hold crucial evidence about how she got there."

"So you think it's a crime scene, miss?"

"It may well be. But as she's clearly still alive, the priority is to apply first aid. Tommy, could you please run down the High Street and fetch Dr Perkins, if he's at home? Tell him it's an emergency."

"He's bound to be at home since he retired last month." Billy's tone was grudging. "And him only sixty, too."

"Then can we call an ambulance?" asked Tommy, hopefully. The appearance of any emergency services vehicle in the village was always a cause for excitement and gossip.

"We'll let Dr Perkins be the judge of that," I said, wary of making false accusations, and of frightening the children. I hoped there might be an innocent explanation for Bunny Carter's dilemma. "Besides, he'll get here much faster than an ambulance, especially now the humpback bridge on the Slate Green road is closed for repair. They'll have to go the long way round. Those first few minutes could be crucial."

Sina grabbed her brother's sleeve. "I'll come with you, Tommy."

Billy followed them through the lychgate. "I'd better go and fetch Kitty, if I can persuade her to leave the house."

"What about me?" I called, alarmed at the prospect of being left alone with the body, even if it was still alive. "And who's Kitty, anyway?"

Billy shouted back over his shoulder to me. "Just keep an eye on Bunny and make sure she doesn't try to get out of that hole by herself."

I hugged myself for comfort, unsure what to do in the meantime. Then, ashamed of my faint heart when an old lady might be dying in front of me, I crept forward and peered into the grave again. She looked surprisingly peaceful, and she was certainly wrapped up warm.

Amid the stillness, a sudden loud fluttering and a rush of air at my back made me cry out in alarm. I looked round to see a large black crow alight on the grass before stalking confidently over to the nearest floral tribute, where it began pecking vigorously at the roses, seeking insects among the petals. I tried not to think of dead sheep's eyes.

Then it occurred to me that we might not be alone. If Bunny Carter hadn't entered the grave of her own accord, her assailant might be lurking behind a gravestone, preparing to despatch any witnesses. The open grave was deep enough to take me too, and Billy, Tommy, and Sina, come to that. I pictured us piled unceremoniously on top of each other, limbs sprawling, heads lolling, like the cover illustration on a book about the Black Death that I'd just shelved in our children's history section.

What method might her attacker have used? There was no sign of a weapon, nor of any blood.

Stubbing my toe against the scythe that Billy had left lying on the ground, I realised its sturdy handle could deal a hefty enough blow to the head of an elderly lady. Might Billy—? No, I couldn't believe he would do such a thing to his own aunt.

I looked about me for tell-tale footprints. There were footprints everywhere in the dew on the grass, from the children's earlier antics and Billy's labours, as well as from our recent arrival. It was anyone's guess whether another party had been through, with or without Bunny Carter. There were also strange parallel lines in the turf, weaving in and out of the tombstones, as if a figure skater had been practising fancy manoeuvres between the graves.

Following their trail to the edge of the churchyard, I jumped at the sight of a new feature I'd not seen before. Against the wall, bathed in a shaft of sunlight like a spotlight from heaven, stood a dove-grey marble slab bearing my surname. For a split second, my heart stood still, until I realised the name etched above it was not mine but my aunt's. Auntie May's headstone had at last been installed.

When I first came to live in the village the previous June on inheriting her cottage, I'd been upset to discover May's grave was marked only by a small wooden cross no bigger than a bookmark, hand-lettered in blunt pencil with her name and date of death.

When, in floods of tears, I phoned my father at my parents' home in Inverness, he had explained that after a burial, the freshly-dug soil must be left to settle before a headstone can be installed, or else it will sit crooked or fall over. The monumental mason in Slate Green would install hers when the time was right.

I tramped across the grass and crouched down to read the rest of the inscription. Its gilded lettering glittered in the sunshine. As I traced the words chiselled beneath May's name, their sharp edges grazed my fingertip:

"*'Tis a better thing to travel hopefully than to arrive.*"

I smiled. I didn't need Hector to tell me that was a quote from Robert Louis Stevenson, one of my travel-writer aunt's favourite authors. What would St Peter make of her attitude when she pitched up at the pearly gates?

I resolved to return later with some flowers for her grave – not shop-bought ones, or wreaths, such as those which lay on some of the plots nearby, but something gathered from her beloved garden that I was now doing my best to tend in her memory. Her garden was also proving a source of inspiration for my own attempts at literature, mainly my monthly column in the parish magazine under the title "Travels with my Aunt's Garden".

Yes, as May could no longer spend time in her garden, I'd move the mountain to Mohammed.

Then my reverie was cut short by a long, eerie moan.

3 Doctor's Orders

For a moment, I thought it was Auntie May calling me from beneath the turf, but the sound was coming from behind me. Bunny Carter was rallying.

I dashed back to kneel beside the open grave, peering down into its depths for signs of movement. While her breathing was not strong enough to make the heavy fabric of her fur coat rise and fall, she was definitely beginning to regain consciousness.

I shouted down into the hole. "Don't worry, Mrs Carter, help is on its way. Just lie still. The doctor will be here soon. Until then I'll look after you."

A skinny hand reached out from within a furry sleeve to twitch acknowledgement.

Just then, the lychgate clicked open, signalling the arrival of the doctor, carrying his black bag, and followed by Tommy and Sina. I was relieved that Dr Perkins was willing to attend despite his retirement. He even looked pleased that we'd summoned him. After a lifetime of doctoring, perhaps he was missing his old routine. Would I ever find a job that brought the same satisfaction as well as paying the bills? The career I craved as a writer still ranked as an unpaid hobby.

Dr Perkins crouched down beside me to bellow into the grave. "MRS CARTER?" He turned to me apologetically. "Deafness runs in her family."

Tommy and Sina stood on the opposite side of the hole, Sina hopping about from foot to foot and Tommy clicking his fingers impatiently.

Something within the fur coat stirred, and Bunny's exposed hand twitched once more.

"Good, she's still with us," said the doctor. "But we'd better not move her yet in case anything's broken. Hips, limbs, pelvis, whatever – all quite likely to go at her advanced age." He looked up. "Tommy, please run next door to the vicarage and ask Mrs Murray for some blankets. Mrs Carter may be wearing a nice warm fur coat, but we don't know how long she's been there. Lying motionless on damp soil in the shade could quickly induce hypothermia. Ideally, we should insulate her from the cold ground by putting a blanket underneath her, but I daren't risk moving her till I've checked for broken bones. We can certainly cover her up, though." As Tommy ran off, the doctor turned to me. "Have you any idea how long she's been down there?"

I shook my head. "No, sorry. First I knew was when Sina came running into the shop just now to alert us. She could have been there all morning for all I know. Billy didn't notice her when he was working in the churchyard earlier today, but the open grave would have been covered up." I pointed to the crumpled artificial grass sheet beside the grave.

The doctor removed his jacket and rolled up his shirtsleeves. "I'll go down to check her out while you phone 999 for an ambulance." He pulled his mobile phone from his trouser pocket and gave it to me. "It's the first number on my speed dial list. Sina, once I'm down there, please pass me my black bag."

I hesitated with my finger over the call button. "Just an ambulance? Don't you want the police as well?"

As he ventured carefully down the ladder, he sent a shower of dirt across Bunny's fur coat. "My dear Sophie, this is a medical matter, not a crime scene."

I wasn't yet convinced that foul play wasn't involved, but bowed to the doctor's greater experience.

"It's probably just a case of her disobeying my advice not to venture out unaccompanied," he continued. "I don't know what her daughter was thinking, letting her go out alone."

"And in such an unsuitable outfit too," I said as I waited for the emergency operator to answer. "She'll ruin those pretty slippers wearing them out of doors."

The doctor reached up to receive his medical bag from Sina and pulled out his stethoscope. "Ruining her slippers is the least of her worries."

As I gave our location to the operator, Sina settled down at the end of the grave as if to supervise the proceedings. She dangled her skinny legs over the edge, drumming her heels against the dark earth walls. Crumbs of rich soil fluttered like confetti on to the doctor's back.

Just as the operator told me an ambulance was on its way, Tommy raced back with a pile of crocheted blankets and threw them down into the grave. One landed over the doctor's head, like a hunter's net trapping a wild animal in a pit. The doctor swatted it crossly away as he put his stethoscope to Bunny's chest. We all fell silent. I held my breath.

"I've got a steady heartbeat," he said after a few moments.

"Yes, but what about hers?" said Tommy.

17

I was still wondering how and why Bunny Carter had got into the grave in the first place.

"Why did she come here? Was she in the habit of going for a solitary stroll?"

The doctor pulled the earpieces from his ears, leaving the stethoscope dangling round his neck like a mayor's chain of office.

"Not lately. When she was steadier on her feet, she used to go for regular walks on her own around the village to be sociable. Then when she became too frail to go alone, Billy would accompany her."

"Is Billy her carer?"

If so, that was news to me.

The doctor pressed his lips together as if about to give bad news. "No. Her daughter Kitty has been, ever since she came back to live with her mother some years ago."

He reached into his bag for a digital thermometer. "Not long ago, one of her sons, Paul, bought her a wheelchair, and Billy offered to take her out in it."

"Why didn't Kitty?"

"Kitty seldom leaves the house. But Bunny said if she couldn't go out on her own two feet, she wouldn't go at all. So she hasn't been anywhere beyond her own garden walls for years."

He inserted the thermometer into Bunny's right ear. "She's done well to get to this age without needing frequent trips to hospital or even to the GP."

"Strong genes?" I asked. He gave me a cynical look.

"Lucky enough to have a family doctor still prepared to make house calls." He pointed to himself. "I don't know whether my replacement will be as obliging. However, she's about to start making up for lost time. I need to get her into hospital and on a drip as soon as possible."

18

He looked at his watch and raised his voice to speak to her again.

"Are you in any pain, Mrs Carter? I don't think you've broken any bones, but there's some nasty bruising."

She didn't reply.

"Mrs Carter, did your daughter bring you here today?"

Silence.

He straightened up to speak to me again. "In one way, if this was Kitty's doing, it would be a good thing, as it would mean she was getting over her agoraphobia. But it would be pretty damning of her suitability as a carer."

"Whoever it was, they must have had some form of transport to get her here," I said. "I wonder what they used?"

"Her wheelchair, obviously," said Sina brightly. "We wondered what that wheelchair was doing here."

"Where is it, then?" said the doctor, stepping on to the ladder and popping his head up to look around at ground level like a meerkat.

Sina pointed to the compost heap in the far corner of the churchyard. From behind a mountain of rotting weeds and dried-out bramble cuttings, a single aluminium wheel glinted in the sun. A wheelchair would account for the tramlines in the grass, especially if wielded by two lively young people like Tommy and Sina.

"We found it this morning when we got here after breakfast," said Sina. "To start with, it was good fun, but Tommy got fed up after I tipped him out accidentally on purpose, so he stuck it on the compost to get it out of the way. Then Billy came, so we helped him for a bit. Then we decided to play hide and seek, and Tommy moved the fake grass out of the way so he could get into the grave. And that's when we found the Easter Bunny."

"Moved the fake grass?" I echoed. "Even if Bunny had come to the churchyard alone and climbed down the ladder into the grave, she couldn't have reached to pull the fake grass across the top of it once she was inside. Someone else must have done that. But why?"

Tommy ignored my question. "An empty grave usually makes a very good hiding place," he said. "But the Easter Bunny beat me to it."

"Oh, for goodness' sake, how old are you two?" The doctor wagged a finger at them. "If you'd have looked properly, you'd have easily seen it wasn't the Easter Bunny, but a human being, and you could have fetched me sooner. Every minute makes a difference in a situation like this."

"I'm always better at hiding than seeking," Tommy admitted, his face falling.

The doctor did not relent. "Besides, didn't you wonder who the wheelchair belonged to?"

Sina shrugged. "How am I supposed to know? It's none of my business. People leave things here all the time. It's not like this is my back garden. But I did notice it said 'The Manor House, WB' on the back of the seat."

"Well done, Sina, that means it must be Mrs Carter's." I spoke in a gentler tone than the doctor. As a trained teacher, I'm much more attuned than Dr Perkins to what motivates children to cooperate. "Now, are you sure you didn't see Mrs Carter sitting in the wheelchair at any time? Nor anyone else? Whatever you tell me, I promise no-one will be cross with either of you. Tommy, are you sure you hadn't been paid to take her out in it?"

Tommy, an instinctive entrepreneur, offered dog-walking services in exchange for pocket money, so adding granny-walking to his repertoire would not have surprised me. He could be reckless too. One false step beside an open grave with an unstable wheelchair, and—

"No, honest, miss, I never."

Sina sprang to her brother's defence. "No, Sophie, he honestly didn't. Anyway, Mrs Carter's still alive, so I don't know why you're complaining."

The doctor coughed. "Yes, she's alive all right. Always a good outcome after a doctor's visit. But whoever abandoned her here has some tricky questions to answer. Leaving an elderly lady outdoors alone in a solitary place, even upright in a wheelchair, amounts to serious neglect."

Tommy stared at me. "More likely someone's tried to murder her. Especially since they replaced the fake grass afterwards. It's like they didn't want her to be found."

Sina shook her head. "Maybe the grass was meant to keep her warm while they went for help. Or she did it herself to make a den. I like making dens, don't I, Tommy?" She peered down into the hole again. "A grave would make a good den, if you put a few cushions and snacks down there. And took a torch and a blanket and a good book. If that's what it's like to be dead and buried, maybe it's not as bad as people make out."

"That's enough speculation from you two," said the doctor, more brusquely than they deserved. "Now, run along and play somewhere else, somewhere a bit more appropriate, such as the playpark. It's a glorious day, so make the most of the sunshine before the weather breaks."

I looked up at the cloudless blue sky.

"And Sophie, no need for you to stay here either. I'll deal with the emergency services when they arrive. And no doubt Hector will be wanting you back at work."

"Are you sure you don't want me to call the police before I go?"

"Or the fire brigade to winch her to the surface," said Tommy. "And how about mountain rescue? If they bring ropes, I could abseil down into the grave to help you."

"What's wrong with using the ladder?" I said, trying not to laugh. "Besides, I don't think we have a branch of mountain rescue in the Cotswolds We've no mountains."

Tommy was undaunted. "Perhaps I should start one up."

The doctor straightened the blankets over Bunny and passed his bag up to Sina. "Actually, Tommy, I'm sure this will all turn out to be a simple domestic issue between Bunny and Kitty. No need to make a drama out of it. The paramedics will be quite sufficient without calling in our boys in blue, or anyone else for that matter."

I held the top of the ladder steady as he clambered out of the grave.

"Boys in blue? Why blue?" asked Sina. "Does wearing blue clothes make you think better?" She looked down in disappointment at her purple top with its pink sequinned flamingo.

"He means the police," said Tommy. Then he beamed at me. "But who needs the police when you've got us to solve the mystery, eh, miss?"

The doctor brushed loose earth off his trousers.

"So are you self-appointed Neighbourhood Watch now, Tommy?"

"We don't just watch," said Tommy proudly. "We do things, don't we, miss?"

4 Door to Door

"What have you done with Billy?" Hector kept his voice low so as not to be overheard by browsing customers. For the sake of confidentiality, I went to join him behind the trade counter.

"He went to fetch Kitty, Bunny's daughter. She's also her carer."

"I know who Kitty is, thank you. I see Bunny and Kitty most weeks when I deliver their book orders."

"Yes, of course. Though I confess I wouldn't recognise either of them if I saw them in the street, even though they live next door but one to me, in the Manor House."

"Anyone as new to the village as you are probably would never have seen Bunny out and about, nor Kitty. The Carters keep themselves to themselves behind the high garden walls of that big old house. Why do you think I always take her books to her house rather than her coming to the shop? Though I admit, I enjoy her company. She's a feisty old stick."

I thought for a moment. "Do you think she wore the bunny ears as a means of identification? So that anyone who didn't know her by sight might at least guess her name?"

Hector looked scornful. "It would have been easier to wear a name badge, or to carry a piece of ID on her, such as her purse. Still, I'm glad Bunny's survived her ordeal intact. An alarming number of elderly people die after a fall."

"Do you really think it could have been an innocent accident? I don't."

He frowned. "It's certainly odd. What did Billy make of it?"

"He seemed cross with her at first, as if she was just up to mischief."

"Did he persuade Kitty to come to the churchyard?"

"I don't know. They hadn't come back by the time I left. I hope they got there before the paramedics arrived. No doubt Kitty would want to go in the ambulance with her mother. In the meantime, Dr Perkins stayed to wait for the paramedics, so Bunny was in safe hands."

It wasn't the first time I'd seen the doctor in action in a village emergency. "He couldn't have been more caring. He even got down into the grave with her. But he clearly wanted us out of the way before the ambulance arrived."

"I'm not surprised. Medical examinations aren't a spectator sport. She might be an old lady, but she still deserves to be treated with dignity. Besides, I wouldn't put it past Tommy and Sina to try to stow away in the ambulance."

As if I'd summoned it up, an ambulance whisked past the shop, blue lights flashing, sirens blaring. Customers looked up from the books they were browsing and began speculating about its mission.

"Must be serious if they've got the sirens on," said a lady in the cookery section.

"Poor soul, whoever it is," said a man in maps.

At that point, Billy stumbled in, stern-faced, followed by Tommy. Sina must have taken the doctor's advice to go to the playpark.

"I call that downright rude," said Billy. "They couldn't even wait for me to get back before they took her off. Me, her own nephew!"

Several customers whispered about this clue as to the passenger's identity.

"Go and help yourself to a cookie, Tommy," I said, so we could speak out of his earshot. Then I turned to Billy. "Nor Kitty either? She must be pretty miffed."

Billy leaned towards us across the trade counter.

"Between you and me, I couldn't raise Kitty. I stood knocking at her front door, shouting like a fool, and she didn't answer. Even deaf old Joshua next door came out to see what the racket was."

"Maybe she'd gone out," I suggested. "And Bunny escaped in her absence."

"Bunny's not exactly held prisoner," said Hector.

"Besides, Kitty never leaves the house," said Billy. "She doesn't like the outdoors, not since a nasty encounter at some festival a few years ago. That's why she came back to live with her mother. She was in there all right. I tracked her down indoors eventually." He lowered his voice. "But now I'm worried she might be back to her old tricks with the sleeping pills."

I gasped. "She drugged her mother?" I'd pictured Kitty as a gentle, harmless person because of her sweet old-fashioned name.

Billy edged closer to me. "No, drugged herself. We all thought she'd got over her old problem, and good thing too, because if she relapses, she won't be allowed to look after her mother no more."

Hector's brow furrowed. "That's a serious accusation, Billy. Are you sure?"

Billy shrugged. "Maybe."

Tommy returned, crunching a gingerbread man and dropping a trail of crumbs in his wake. "Wow, how did you get into her house, then? Did you have to smash the door down? I'd have helped if you'd asked me."

I bet he would. I wanted to remind them both that this would have been a criminal act. "You broke in? I hope no-one saw you."

"What do you take me for, girlie? I've got me own key to the Manor House. Me being Kitty's cousin, she says it makes her feel safer knowing I could let myself in if there was an emergency. Mind you, I couldn't find my key just now. Must have left it in my other jacket, the one I was wearing when I was there gardening yesterday. So I went round the back and climbed in the open kitchen window."

"So was Kitty okay?" I asked.

He shook his head. "The house was quiet as the grave, and as soon as I was in, I found out why. There she was, with her head on the kitchen table."

Tommy's mouth fell open. "Where was the rest of her?"

Billy tutted. "I mean she was sitting at the kitchen table and had rested her head on it for a nap. I gave her a good shake, but she was out for the count. She must have been up for hours, as the pot of tea she'd made for herself was half drunk but stone cold."

He sighed. "So I've left her to sleep it off, and I'll go back in a while to make her some coffee and a sandwich to get her back on an even keel. She wouldn't have been no use to her mother in that condition. But I don't want to go drawing attention to it, so you keep it to yourselves, or else folk will say she's not fit to be her mother's carer, and that would break both their hearts. And don't tell Dr Perkins, whatever you do."

Half expecting him to spit on his palm to shake on the deal, I was relieved when he kept his hands in his pockets.

"We don't want nothing said against Kitty," he continued. "Otherwise that bullying brother of hers, Paul, will be putting Bunny in one of his care homes and turning Kitty out on her ear."

A creak at the shop door heralded the arrival of Dr Perkins. He marched straight past us to wash his hands at the sink in the tearoom with the thoroughness of a pre-op surgeon and dried them on the nearest tea towel. I made a mental note to put it straight into the laundry basket when he'd gone.

Then he sat down at an empty tearoom table. "I think I've earned a cappuccino, don't you, Sophie?"

Billy came over to sit opposite him. "What's your prognosis for my Auntie Bunny, Doc?"

"I'll tell you what I can after my coffee," said the doctor.

As I dropped the first capsule into the coffee machine, Hector joined them, while Tommy hovered hopefully nearby, till the doctor spotted him.

"Tommy, well done for raising the alarm this morning," he said, and the boy grew taller with pride. "Now, how would you like to do another good deed for the day? Could you fetch that old wheelchair from the churchyard and return it to the Manor House? Don't go bothering Kitty. Just leave it in the porch. They might need it when Bunny comes home from hospital."

The doctor reached into his pocket and pulled out a couple of pound coins. "And here's some money to buy sweets from the shop. But only once you've done it, mind."

"Wow, thanks, Doc," said Tommy, beaming. "You can rely on me."

Dr Perkins waited till Tommy had left the shop before continuing. "Patient confidentiality forbids me from telling you the details, but I'm pretty sure Bunny Carter will pull through. She's made of stern stuff. I have a copy of the paramedics' report, which I shall drop in to Kitty now. I'm guessing you couldn't persuade her to leave the house, Billy?"

Billy's eyes widened. "You could say that, Doc. You know what she's like."

The doctor sighed. "I do wish she'd drop this silly charade about being agoraphobic so she can visit her mother in hospital. They're bound to keep Bunny in at least overnight for observation, even if the x-rays confirm my diagnosis that she's not broken any bones. It'll take a day or two for the bruising to come out. She'll probably end up looking as if she's been in a punch-up."

"I'll drop the report off for you if you like, Doc, to save your legs," said Billy hastily. "I'm going back up to the Manor House in a minute."

The doctor raised his eyebrows. "The paramedics entrusted it to me. It's my responsibility to deliver it to Kitty as next of kin."

He produced the neatly folded report from his inside jacket pocket and held it up as evidence.

"Patient confidentiality again, I suppose," I said, hoping to save Billy embarrassment.

"I'm almost as much her kin as Kitty is," said Billy. "What's wrong, is there something on the report that you don't want me to see?"

"Nothing, nothing," replied the doctor.

"Oh well, don't rush your coffee, Doc," said Billy. "No point in hurrying to be the bearer of bad news. Allow the poor woman to remain in blissful ignorance a little longer."

He sat back in his chair, clasped his hands behind his head, and began to whistle a leisurely tune.

"By the way, how did Kitty take the news?" asked the doctor. "Had she realised that Bunny had gone out on her own? But wait, what am I thinking, lingering here over coffee when she may be having a panic attack? I ought to get up there straight away. Delivering the paramedics' report will give me the excuse I need to call on her."

He began to gulp down his coffee, though it must have been too hot to drink comfortably.

Billy stared. "Don't you worry, Doc. She was very relaxed when I left her."

I nearly choked on my own coffee at his smooth cover-up of Kitty's incapacity.

"I'll be there for the rest of the day, working on her garden," he continued. "I'll keep an eye on her."

"Yes, but you're not a medical professional," said the doctor, scraping back his chair. "I'm only doing my duty. Well, not official duty. I keep forgetting I've retired. But if not duty, conscience calls. It's really no problem. I had nothing else planned today."

"What about insurance?" asked Hector, ever practical. "If you're retired now, are you still insured to practise? Don't let your kind heart get you into trouble."

"Oh, for goodness' sake, Hector, it's not as if I'm giving her brain surgery. I'm being little more than a messenger."

Billy stood up. "Well, they shoot messengers, don't they? But I'm family. You give it to me, Doc. If you don't want me to read it, just put it in an envelope. Hector, you must have envelopes behind that desk of yours, haven't you?"

Billy whisked the paramedics' report from the doctor's grasp while Hector scurried behind the counter to fetch an envelope. Billy stuffed the report inside it, licked the flap to seal it, and slid it into his trouser pocket.

"I'll be off, then. And don't worry, Doc, Kitty's younger than both of us. She'll be fine."

The doctor pursed his lips. "After a lifetime in my profession, I can tell you that illness and death are no respecters of age. There's no pecking order. Life's not like taking a pleasure boat out on a lake: 'Come in, number 93, your time is up.' You know that from the graves you've dug over the years, Billy."

"More coffee, doctor?" I said brightly, buying time for Kitty as Billy headed for the door. "It's on the house."

5 Ham-Fisted

As the number of customers dwindled towards lunchtime, Hector put Stravinsky's *Rites of Spring* on the sound system and came over to the tearoom to join me for lunch. Just as we started to eat our sandwiches, there came a knock at the shop window. Hector laughed and pointed. Tommy, seated in Bunny's wheelchair, was waving cheerfully at us as he propelled himself down the High Street in the direction of the Manor House. He was having fun.

"He makes it look easy," said Hector, "but Bunny wouldn't have the strength to do that."

I picked up a spoon to stir my coffee. "I'm glad whoever wheeled her down there had the sense to wrap her up in a fur coat. At her age, she'll feel the cold. But why those ridiculous bunny ears?"

I passed Hector the spoon.

"Spring fever? An eccentric old lady's whim to entertain passing children? She's very fond of children. Though that doesn't explain the pink slippers."

I waved my hand dismissively. "The slippers don't need explaining. Old people's feet swell up easily, and

31

they like comfy slippers. In a wheelchair, she wouldn't need outdoor shoes."

I took a sip of coffee. "Who else helps look after her? Does she have any other carers besides Kitty and Billy? If it was an accident or a domestic dispute, as the doctor seems to think, maybe someone other than Kitty was responsible. A new and inexperienced carer might have persuaded her to go out in the wheelchair for once, but then lost control of it. They might have tipped her into the grave by mistake, then gone to fetch help."

Hector took a mouthful of tea. "Not unless they've arrived in the last week, since my most recent delivery to the Manor House, or Bunny would have told me about them. And if they went to get help, they took their time about it. And where are they now? Don't forget Tommy and Sina were playing with the empty wheelchair for some time before they discovered the body. It wouldn't take that long for someone to fetch help."

I nodded. "Besides, most people these days carry a mobile phone, so they'd be more likely to ring for help rather than abandoning the poor old soul to fend for herself in a grave."

He set down his cup. "And if their phone battery was flat, they could have shouted for help to the next person passing by on the High Street. It's not as if they were in an isolated spot."

I grimaced. "Perhaps they just panicked. If they thought they'd accidentally killed her, they might have run off to hide."

Hector picked up the second half of his sandwich. "I suppose one of her other children might have come to see her and persuaded her to take a spin in the wheelchair."

"How many children does she have?"

"About ten, I think, from her three marriages."

"Ten children? My goodness!"

Hector grinned. "How do you think she acquired the nickname Bunny? Endless reproducing in her younger days. My dad told me she was a once bit of a goer."

"No wonder she's too tired to go out now."

Hector laughed, then turned more serious. "Sadly, only the two boys from her second marriage, Paul and Stuart, still live locally, and they're down in Slate Green. I know them to say hello to, but that's about all. I think they're the only ones she has any contact with these days, apart from Kitty, the youngest. A few of the others emigrated to Australia, and the rest are scattered about the country."

"My goodness, how awful to have such a large family, but lose so many one way or another." As an only child, I could barely imagine her sense of loss. "What about the husbands? Are they all dead?"

"I hope so, because they're all buried in the churchyard. If you want chapter and verse on them, ask Joshua. He and Bunny are about the same age. They probably went to school together." He put the remains of his sandwich on his plate for a moment. "Nice ham, this."

I popped a stray sliver into my mouth. "I know, I keep thinking about going vegetarian, but every time I see Carol's lovely ham in the village shop, I postpone the idea."

"Bunny's just gone vegetarian, and made Kitty do it too, though I got the impression Kitty wasn't keen."

"How do you know that?" I asked.

"Bunny asked me to take a very expensive vegetarian cookery book round to her a few months ago. I had to order it in specially. The shop does well out of Bunny Carter, considering she never sets foot in it."

I swallowed hastily, not wanting to speak with my mouth full. "But if they're both vegetarians, what on earth was Bunny doing wearing a fur coat?"

Hector stared at me. "Good God, you're right. Bunny is vehement about animal cruelty, and her vegetarianism is only the tip of the iceberg. On her kitchen table are piles of letters from every animal charity imaginable. She told me she doesn't open most of them as she can't bear to read about animals suffering, or to see the horrific pictures. She just keeps sending money to the charities in the hope of making it stop."

I frowned. "So Bunny would never wear a fur coat. Perhaps it was someone's idea of a practical joke."

"A cruel one in appalling taste," said Hector.

"If it wasn't her fur coat, I wonder whose it was?" As I spoke, I remembered noticing a dry-cleaning label attached to the sleeve with a safety pin. I kicked myself for not checking the name, but at that point I'd assumed it to be her own. "Poor Bunny. Why would anyone want to be so unkind to an innocent old lady?"

Hector grinned. "Being an old lady doesn't make you innocent. She's got up to all sorts of mischief in her time, playing her children off against each other something rotten. For example, she's refused to tell Kitty what's in her will. She was just as much a tease to her three husbands, too."

"Oh my! Not all at once, surely? Or do you mean she was a bigamist? Or is it a trigamist, if you've got three husbands at once?"

He laughed. "No, she only married one at a time, and each died of natural causes. So don't go jumping to any conclusions about her being a serial husband-assassin, although rumour has it the second and third were lined up on a promise before their predecessor was cold. She married each of them within months of being widowed."

"She was probably keen to secure a provider for her growing brood of children," I said. "Women had to be more pragmatic about marriage in those days."

I recalled the wizened figure swamped by the fur coat, trying to picture what she must have looked like when she was young and beautiful.

The door swung wide open, and a babble of eager voices filled the shop as a family of regular customers entered. The four children scurried to different age-appropriate shelves, and the mum to the historical fiction section, while the dad sauntered over to our table to catch up with Hector.

"Back to work," said Hector cheerfully, as he pushed back his chair and got up to speak to him. "Hi, Hugh, I've got just the book for you – a stunning collection of aerial views of the mountains of the world. The Battersby rep brought in a copy this morning."

Hugh's dark eyes lit up. "That blonde woman who was in here last week when I came in? The one who brings you presents."

Hector grinned. "The very same. She is lovely, isn't she?"

Hugh winked at him. "She must be keen if she visits you on a Saturday. Going for the more mature type now, are you?"

Hector let that comment go unremarked. "Now, let me find that book for you," he said, leaving me to clear away our lunch things.

So, the Battersby rep was some gorgeous blonde, was she? And while most reps visited quarterly or monthly at most, her visits had become weekly, and in her own time at weekends? No wonder Hector had been so keen to get me out of the shop when she was due earlier that morning. The previous Saturday morning he'd despatched me to the Post Office to post a parcel. I'd wondered why we'd started stocking so many of Battersby's huge, colourful coffee-table books, far beyond the unit price of our average sale. Hector had slapped a '£10 off RRP' sticker on every one, so they wouldn't have been making us much profit. Perhaps he was just trying to shift the stock quickly to give the rep an excuse for another visit.

I gazed down at my half-eaten sandwich. Suddenly I'd gone right off ham.

6 Cousinly Love

I'd decided to continue my enquiries after work with a strategic call on my next-door neighbour, Joshua, but I didn't need to wait that long for more gossip about Bunny. As I walked home past the village shop just after five, Carol beckoned me inside.

"I've been hearing all day long about this business with poor Bunny Carter," she hissed before I'd even closed the door behind me. "What a palaver! And wearing my Easter bunny ears, too. She's my cousin, you know. Admittedly a very distant cousin, but some kind of relation. I don't know where she got those ears from. Certainly not from me. Whatever was she thinking at her age?"

"It does seem a bit odd, even for Wendlebury."

When she shot me a reproving look, I realised I needed to live longer in the village to gain licence to make fun of it. After all, I'd only moved in the previous summer. Some days it felt like much longer.

"Maybe someone was trying to frame you," I said in jest. "Everyone in the village would recognise those ears as your handiwork."

Carol was not amused. "Why would anyone suggest I'd be so cruel to poor Bunny?"

"Rich Bunny, actually," said a voice from the back of the shop. It was Bob, the policeman who lived a few doors up from Hector's House. "She's got to be pretty rich living in that big house. She inherited it from her third husband, and everyone said he was loaded. My mum said that's why Bunny married him, to get a big house for all her kids." He spoke without malice or envy, just as a statement of record.

"You make her sound like the old woman who lived in a shoe," I said.

He grinned. "Apparently she was a bit, when they all lived at home with her. But it's a fabulous house. There's plenty of people who'd like to get their hands on it when she passes. Like Paul, for a start."

"Bunny's son, Paul?" Encouraging a serving police officer to gossip felt naughty, but I told myself I was only establishing the facts.

"One of her sons. He's got his own building company and also runs care homes for a living, develops and builds them, too. It's no secret that he's got his eye on the Manor House to add to his empire when his mother dies. Not that it'll necessarily go to him. Bunny likes to keep people guessing about who she's leaving it to."

Carol put one hand to her cheek in thought. "Wendlebury could do with a care home. Then the old people wouldn't have to leave the village when they get too inert to look after themselves."

"You mean infirm," I corrected her gently. "It would save them having to depend on the next generation, too." Carol had spent her prime looking after her ailing mother at home. "I don't know what it's like on the inside, but from the outside it looks as if it would make

38

an excellent care home, after a bit of tarting up. It seems a bit run down."

"Yes, but not while Bunny's still in it," said Carol. "Paul shouldn't be pushing her out of it for the sake of his business interests."

"I've heard she doesn't make best use of it," said Bob, coming to join us and placing his shopping on the counter – his usual essentials: a four-pack of lager, a bag of dry-roasted peanuts and a large bar of chocolate. "I see Paul in Slate Green occasionally, when I'm at work, and we've had the odd pint together. He told me that Bunny and Kitty hardly use any of the rooms, and the rest of it is falling down about their ears. I can see his point of view. He's offered to do it up and give her and Kitty a room each, and all their needs would be catered for – meals, laundry, entertainment."

"Kitty's not old enough to be in a care home yet, surely?" I'd pictured her as a young woman, but if Bunny was Joshua's contemporary, even as her youngest child, Kitty could be around retirement age.

"Pushing sixty, I'd say," said Bob.

"They let them into these places very young these days," said Carol.

Bob winked at me. "Yes, you might like to apply yourself, Sophie."

Carol started to ring up his purchases on the till. "Well, perhaps if Paul just asked her nicely rather than trying to push her into it, she might agree. Perhaps it was him that tipped her into the grave to teach her a lesson. That's the sort of thing a bully would do. It's downright wicked, even if she was knocked out first with sleeping pills. A fall like that could give an old lady a nasty haemorrhoid."

I put my hand over my mouth to hide my smile. "I think you mean haemorrhage."

Bob took a step back, his face serious. "How do you know she was on sleeping pills?"

Carol pointed to a large white plastic box, stowed out of reach of customers behind the counter, bearing the logo of the Slate Green pharmacy. It held the medicines they delivered regularly, along with a signing sheet for patients or their representatives to acknowledge safe receipt. This service saved villagers a journey to the dispensary in town.

Bob frowned. "That's why the dispenser packages the medicines in sealed paper bags, so no-one else beside the patient and the doctor knows what's inside." He paled. "Do you know what's in my prescription?"

I bit my lip, trying not to think about what that might be. Carol diverted her gaze, pretending to concentrate on putting his shopping into a flimsy plastic carrier bag.

"Of course not," she said briskly, inadvertently making a hole in the bag with the corner of the chocolate bar. "Kitty must have just mentioned the nature of Bunny's medication when I took it down to her one day. Or Billy. He sometimes delivers her prescriptions to save me the bother, when he goes in to do their gardening."

Here was a good opportunity for me to introduce myself to Kitty – and to Bunny, when and if she came home from hospital.

"I don't mind dropping them in for you any time. It's hardly out of my way."

"Thank you, Sophie, that would be very kind, and I'm sure you'll be more reliable than Billy," said Carol. She seemed relieved to have the conversation back on a more businesslike track. "I think I've got a new prescription for her that came in just yesterday. You just need to sign for them on her behalf."

She delved into the front of the box in which the bags were neatly filed in alphabetical order by patient's name. Carol liked order. Her whole shop is stocked in alphabetical order by product.

"Actually, no, I haven't." She held up the clipboard. "It's on my list all right, but someone must have signed for them when Becky was covering for my lunch hour yesterday." Becky is her grown-up daughter, about my age, who recently came with her baby son Arthur to live with Carol.

Carol held the list out at arm's length to scrutinise the signature. "It looks like Billy's already taken them."

7 Joshua's Clues

I'd expected Joshua to be more upset by Bunny's accident, because it would remind him of his own frailty. Instead, he seemed positively jocular. Perhaps he felt like fighter pilots used to in wartime after a colleague had been killed, secretly glad not to be that day's statistic.

"Perhaps she'd gone down to put flowers on her husband's grave and tripped up," he said.

That seemed unlikely, given that everyone said she'd hardly been out of the house for years, but I was glad of the excuse to discuss her marriages.

"Which of the three? Did she have a favourite?"

As I settled down on his sofa, I pictured gold, silver and bronze awards on the husbands' graves.

Joshua let out a low chuckle. "All of them, and some other women's, too."

I laughed. "Hector told me she was a charmer when she was young."

"What you might call a Pied Piper of men."

With tremulous hands, he handed me a delicate vintage glass of sloe gin before returning to his fireside armchair.

"Yes, she was a charmer, as her husbands would readily attest. And she had more lined up to take their place should another vacancy arise."

My eyes widened. "Didn't the rate of attrition put her other men off?"

Joshua gazed wistfully at the black and white photo of Edith, his late wife, on the mantlepiece.

"You never saw her in all her youthful glory. She was a stunner. Her children, too, when they were young, and all of them so alike."

I tasted the sloe gin and licked my lips. "How odd when they had three different fathers."

Joshua's eyes twinkled again. "Fortunately, none of them turned out looking like me."

I clapped my hand to my mouth. "You mean—?" I knew Joshua had had a love affair with my Auntie May before his long and happy marriage to Edith, and that it had resumed after he was widowed, but I didn't have him down as a philanderer.

He shook his head. "A poor jest on my part. Suffice to say there were plenty of fellows about the village who keenly watched Bunny's pram at each new arrival, waiting to see how Baby turned out."

I took another sip from my glass and let the viscous liquid coat my tongue. "So what's your theory on how she ended up in that grave today?"

He stared into the distance, out of the front window to the High Street. "I've no idea. But it looks as if someone is about to investigate."

He raised his walking stick from beside his chair to point to where a police car had just parked outside his cottage. A uniformed officer got out, peered at the house name on Joshua's front gate, then got back in to his vehicle. The car drove off slowly, moving the few metres required to reach the Manor House, before its engine went silent, just out of our sight. How a policeman could mistake Joshua's cottage for a manor house was beyond me, but then the police were from Slate Green, so not used to our rural ways. The older houses in Wendlebury don't even have door numbers, which confuses relief postmen no end whenever our usual postie goes on holiday.

I hoped Kitty would by now be in a fit state to help them with their enquiries.

A little later, I let myself out of Joshua's house, leaving him resting in his armchair. Instead of taking my usual shortcut home over the low lavender hedge between our front gardens, I sauntered slowly to the end of his path to check whether the police car was still outside the Manor House.

It was, but now there were three people in the car instead of the two officers who had driven past earlier. I couldn't identify the extra passenger until the driver executed a three-point turn. Pretending not to be watching, I dodged back up my own front path, walking as slowly as I could to my front door, turning only as the police car passed my gate.

On the back seat, with his face pressed against the window, and waving desperately to attract my attention, sat Billy, looking utterly bewildered.

8 Kitty's Cats

Curiosity and compassion trumped my natural reserve, and moments later I found myself knocking on the front door of the Manor House. Beneath the canopy of its imposing Georgian pillared porch, I felt as small and unwelcome as a Borrower.

I almost took the lack of an immediate answer as an excuse to bolt back to the safety of my cottage. But knowing Kitty was agoraphobic, I told myself she had to be at home. After the visit from the police that resulted in them taking Billy away, whether under arrest or just for questioning, she must have been anxious, even within the supposed safety of her own four walls. I wanted to reassure her, and to find out what was going on.

Knocking again to no effect, I plucked up the courage to tug the old-fashioned bell-pull. A deep clanging echoed from within. If Kitty hadn't heard my knocking, she couldn't fail to hear this thunderous chime, unless she was profoundly deaf. Dr Perkins had said deafness ran in their family.

A scraping sound came from within, followed by a scuffling, which got closer and closer. When the door finally creaked open a few centimetres, a bleary grey eye, partly obscured by an unruly curl of similar shade, peered at me through the crack.

"Yes?" Kitty's low voice was sullen and resentful. She packed a remarkable amount of expression into a single syllable.

"Hello," I began warily. "I'm Sophie. I live the other side of Joshua Hampton from you."

"Yes."

I paused, hoping she might say more, if only to confirm her identity, but she said nothing. I tried again.

"I'm sorry I haven't been round to introduce myself before, but I was worried about you after your mother's accident this morning." I took her nod to acknowledge Bunny as her mother. "I was with her earlier, just after the children found her, and I sent for Dr Perkins."

"Billy told me."

Well, that was progress. At least we were beyond monosyllables.

She edged the door open just enough to reveal both her eyes, a distinctive aquiline nose and a wide, expressionless mouth. Her face pallid from a life lived indoors, she had the look of a marble Roman statue, and not much more animation. In her youth, she must have been beautiful, even if she did have Billy's nose.

"I know who you are," she said suddenly. "You're May Sayers's girl."

"Her niece, actually," I said, wondering whether she was mixing me and Auntie May up with Becky and her mother, Carol. Becky is about my age and had come to live in the village only a few months after I had.

"That's what I said."

What an unreliable witness, I thought. She can't even remember her own words from one sentence to the next.

What chance would there be of getting any sense out of her about Billy? But I had to ask.

"I've just seen Billy being taken away by the police. Is there anything I can do to help?"

"Questioning."

I was just wondering whether she was referring to my behaviour or that of the police when she opened the door wide and beckoned me in. I stepped into the entrance hall before she could change her mind.

As she led me through to the back of the house, I trod carefully between piles of newspapers lining the passageway. Several were topped with scrawny cats washing themselves. In the kitchen, which featured a 1950s linoleum floor and faded 1960s floral wallpaper, more cats were asleep on half a dozen dusty plastic chairs around an ancient Formica-topped table. I felt as if we were interrupting some kind of feline meditation session.

Kitty jerked the back of one chair to tip a chunky tabby on to the floor, which I took as an invitation to take its place. The poor cat squawked in protest as it landed, briefly washed a front paw to hide its embarrassment, then padded away, aloof, into the hall, as if relocating had been its own idea.

Kitty went to stand a few feet away from me, leaning against a cluttered worktop in front of long, tall windows overlooking the rear grounds. With her back to the light, I could hardly see her face.

"Stitched him up," she said abruptly. "The police. They've stitched him up. Billy wasn't doing no harm. Just looking after me after I felt a bit poorly this morning. And the shock about Mother. Coffee?"

She rummaged among the crumpled empty food packages spread across the worktop and produced two mugs.

"Thanks," I said uncertainly.

To my relief, I spotted a modern coffee machine behind her. She popped a capsule into the machine, and a moment later presented me with a mug of steaming Americano before dispensing another for herself. I hoped the steam would sterilise the mug.

A few sips turned her garrulous.

"The police just came to investigate a report of breaking and entering. They didn't seem interested in Mother's accident, of which I knew nothing until Billy woke me up around lunchtime." She indicated a disturbed pile of papers where her head must have rested on the kitchen table. "I don't know why I was asleep. I never sleep during the day, nor much at night, either. I used to have sleeping pills, but my brother took them away. I don't know why the lazy tyke couldn't get his own. I got up early because I was expecting a visitor at eight o'clock. I forget who. But I couldn't stay awake. What day is it?"

She didn't pause for me to reply.

"I don't know why Billy didn't use his key. Nor did the police. They have keys, don't they? Skeleton keys?"

"The police?"

She nodded slightly. "Billy has a key for when he does our garden, but he said he didn't have it with him today. So he knocked on the door, and I didn't answer, so he told me he climbed in the window. So they took him away. But he needn't have broken in at all, because after he'd gone home yesterday, I discovered the front door lock had jammed open, so he could have got in without his key. When I told him, he said he'd fix it for me, but the police wouldn't listen to either of us, even though I told them he's my cousin. I don't think what he did was wrong, do you?"

I shook my head. "Of course not. Billy was just concerned for you. That's why he came straight down here as soon as we found your mother. It was Billy who identified who she was, and his first thought was to come and get you, while we called the doctor."

"He said an ambulance took Mother away."

"Only later. He came to tell you before the ambulance arrived, so that you could come back with him and go in it with her to the hospital, but you were fast asleep."

"But I told you, that's ridiculous. I'm a very light sleeper. I shouldn't have been asleep."

I shrugged, unwilling to take her word over Billy's.

"But why did the police take Billy away? How could that help Mother?"

"I'm afraid I've got no idea."

She closed her eyes and clutched her head, staggering slightly. "Oh my lord, I've a head full of knives."

Worried that she was about to faint, I stood up and led her gently by the arm to the chair I'd just vacated. She slumped down like a string puppet whose wires had been cut.

"So what happened exactly?"

She picked up the envelope that Billy had used for the paramedics' report and held it over her face. "Could you close the shutters, please? This sun's too bright for me." I did as I was told. "Anyway, the police searched his pockets and found my front door key in his jacket. Even then, they still acted as if he'd been lying about why he'd climbed in the window. But Billy wouldn't lie to me. He's family."

Her mouth crumpled, and tears began to spill silently down her cheeks. Beside me, a ginger cat awoke from its slumber and leapt down to rub itself against Kitty's ankles until she kicked it away. I fumbled in my handbag for a packet of tissues, pulled one out and passed it to her.

"I'm sure you're right." When I patted her free hand, she pulled it away as abruptly as if I'd stubbed out a cigarette on it and hauled herself upright once more. "There must be some misunderstanding. Billy's no criminal."

She glanced about her nervously and got up to stand with her back to the wall. "Stuart doesn't trust him."

"Stuart?" I hadn't come across a Stuart in the village. I wondered whether he was her boyfriend.

"One of my brothers. He's an accountant down in Slate Green. He always says Billy is up to no good, hanging round here all the time. He reckons Billy is after Mother's money. I don't think that's true. Billy's not after anybody's money. He's happy with what he's got – his little cottage, his old age pension, his odd jobs. He wouldn't know what to do with more money if he had it." She sank to the floor, her back sliding down against the wall.

Getting up from my chair, I went over to kneel beside her and put my arms around her, expecting her to push me away. Although stiff and self-conscious at first, she began to lean into my embrace, then started to sob uncontrollably on my shoulder.

"I'm sure you're right about Billy." I spoke softly, stroking her hair. "Perhaps for some reason someone else tried to abduct your mother, someone we don't even know."

I still couldn't believe it was an innocent accident.

Kitty stopped crying and pulled away to look me in the eye. "What, you mean like aliens? I suppose that could happen." She got up to fetch her coffee cup, swirling the dregs around and gazing at them as if they

52

might provide guidance. I was starting to gather the kind of festival Kitty used to frequent.

"Not that sort of abduction. I mean, someone might have taken her out in the wheelchair against her will. Not Billy, though. Did Billy tell you your mother was unconscious when we found her? She'd have been a dead weight for whoever took her there." I winced at my unfortunate choice of words. "Anyway, it bore the hallmark of someone with more imagination than Billy. Dressing her up like that didn't seem like something he would do."

She looked blank. "Dressing her up like what? In her Sunday best? Is it Sunday today?"

I stared back. "Didn't Billy tell you? When we found your mother, she was wearing a fur coat and bunny ears, like some weird Easter bunny costume."

"A fur coat? We don't have a fur coat in the house. She used to have one, which she'd been given as a gift decades ago when fur was all the rage. But she ditched it a few months ago, about the same time that she decided we should go vegetarian. God, I could just eat a bacon sandwich right now."

She stared at the floor.

"She made Stuart take the fur coat away, along with all her old leather shoes and handbags. First of all she wanted to give them a funeral and bury them in the garden, as they had once been living creatures, but Stuart said that was too weird and also a waste. So she told him to take them to an animal charity shop."

She waved a hand towards a wall calendar promoting the plight of Chinese bears.

"Stuart said animal charity supporters wouldn't buy fur, so she told him just to get it out of the house and do what he liked with it, and that was the end of that. I've no idea where it ended up." She sniffed and blew her nose feebly. "He always seems skint these days, so he probably sold it and pocketed the proceeds, and good luck to him. Anyway, the point is, Mother doesn't have a fur coat. Only the other day she said she'd rather die than wear fur."

I was afraid she might still do both.

9 Through Rosé-Tinted Glasses

I had to raise my voice to be heard above the hubbub of The Bluebird's lounge bar. "Do you think Billy will be OK?" I wasn't sure whether you could phone the police station for a progress report in the same way you could check on a person in hospital.

Hector set down a chilled bottle of rosé with one hand and two long-stemmed glasses with the other.

"I can't imagine he's got anything to worry about." He sat down on the bench seat opposite me in our usual booth, half filled each glass, and slid one across the table to me. Then he raised the other to clink against mine in a toast to nothing in particular. "They probably weren't arresting him. I expect they just wanted to talk to him about Bunny without Kitty earwigging."

"So he's just helping the police with their enquiries?" I wasn't convinced. He had looked so helpless in the police car that it seemed something else might be at stake. "Is there any chance Billy stands to inherit the Manor House if Bunny dies?"

For the sake of confidentiality, Hector got up and came round to sit beside me.

"I doubt it." He raised his glass to inspect the wine's colour against the light. "I presume she's leaving it to her kids. She told me she's made a will, but I've no idea who will benefit. She's keeping them guessing, playing them off against each other."

"Isn't that just asking for trouble? Especially after she's fallen out with her other four surviving children."

Hector nodded. "It's not the smartest thing to do. I just hope she'll provide well for Kitty, after she's spent the last twenty-odd years caring for her. But leaving Kitty the whole house might be contentious. It would be a huge house for a single person. Even the two of them rattle around in it. Besides, the two sons that she's still on speaking terms with, from her second marriage, are both businessmen, and the type that might go litigious if she left the lot to Kitty."

"Do they live close by?"

"Slate Green."

I took another sip of wine, enjoying the cool floral taste. I didn't want to criticise Kitty, but our encounter that morning had left me concerned for her state of mind.

"If I was an old lady, I wouldn't be very confident being cared for by Kitty," I said eventually. "She didn't seem all there."

Hector laid a hand companionably on my thigh. "She is rather childlike, isn't she? Between you and me, I suspect appointing her as carer was as much to keep her away from the drugs scene as for Bunny's well-being. Cheaper, too, than hiring a professional. Though money might not be an issue with the sons in Slate Green. The elder, Paul, drives a Jag, and Stuart is an accountant."

"Which might make her more likely to leave the Manor House to the local cats' charity."

He grinned. "She's sufficiently wilful. That's one of the reasons I like her so much. She's got spirit."

He raised his glass in a silent toast to the incorrigible Bunny, smiling as he drank.

"No wonder Kitty doesn't seem fond of their cats," I said. "They're potential rivals for her inheritance."

"Poor old Kitty. She must be financially vulnerable – dependent, even." Hector set his glass down neatly on a beer mat. "Even if Bunny did leave Kitty the whole house, she'd have no income for its upkeep. The only job that Kitty's ever had that I know of is taking a ramshackle catering van round to festivals. I expect when Bunny dies, the Manor House will have to be sold."

I wrinkled my nose. "I wonder who would buy a big house like that? Bob said Bunny's son Paul would like to turn it into a care home. Better that than have it go to some weekender, and stand empty most of the year, or to an anti-social rock star who'll throw noisy all-night parties."

We didn't have any of those in Wendlebury, but that wasn't to say it couldn't happen.

Hector chuckled. "Hark at you, Miss Not-Been-Here-A-Year-But-Not-In-My-Back-Yard Sayers!" I frowned. "Still, let's not anticipate Bunny's demise before she's ready for it. Although she may look as frail as a bird, she's got a cast-iron will, and I wouldn't be surprised to see her back home in a day or two. If she's still in hospital tomorrow, I'll go and visit her and take her a good book to keep her out of mischief. Kitty won't visit her, obviously."

"Can I come? I'd like to meet Bunny. Meet her properly, I mean – while she's fully conscious, the right way up, and not down a hole in the ground."

"That would be a better introduction. And I expect for her part she'd like to thank you for coming to her rescue."

I traced a pattern in the condensation droplets on the outside of my glass. "I can't see I did anything material, besides send Tommy for the doctor. I'm not even sure that was the right thing to do, because Dr Perkins has retired. I've been kicking myself for not dialling 999 straight away and asking for the police as well as an ambulance."

"But Dr Perkins got there before the paramedics. His precautions while you were waiting for the ambulance might have saved her life."

I sighed. "I suppose so." Feeling a little chilly, I leaned in closer to Hector for warmth. Although the day had been unseasonably mild, the early dusk was making it clear that summer was still a long way off. "Do you think Kitty will be all right spending the night on her own in that big house? I'm not sure I would."

"I don't suppose she's had to do that for a long time, if ever," said Hector. "Though she has got all those cats for company."

"That's not the same as having a guard dog, though, is it?"

The front door of the pub swung open, and we turned to inspect the new arrival.

"Perhaps she might have a guard dog tonight after all," said Hector. "Or at least a companion marginally less furry than the cats. Here comes Billy." He put up one hand to attract Billy's attention. "Want to join us, Bill? Sit down, mate, I'll get you a pint."

Billy stomped over and slumped on to the bench opposite us, saying nothing. If there hadn't been a table between us, I could have hugged him.

"Billy, I'm so relieved to see you! You had me worried when I saw you going off in the police car like that. I thought you'd been arrested."

I forced a careless laugh as if that was a ridiculous idea. He scowled at me from beneath furrowed eyebrows.

"So did I. It turns out some interfering fool reported me to the police for breaking and entering the Manor House. When the police got there, they came up with some cock and bull story about finding drugs in my jacket pocket."

"Why on earth would they do that?" asked Hector, returning from the bar, a pint of cider in Billy's special tankard in his hand. Billy might have been fond of a drink and a cigarette, but that was the extent of his vices.

He took a long pull on the pint of cider that Hector had set in front of him.

"No idea. But it was just as well they searched my jacket pockets, because they found my key in there, too, which proved why I had climbed in the window. I had to tell them they were looking in my gardening jacket. I'd left my jacket at Kitty's the day before because I was too warm in it after I'd worked up a muck sweat giving her lawn its first mow of the year. It has its own chair in the kitchen."

I bet it did.

He pointed with both hands to his frayed lapels. "My gardening jacket, I mean, as opposed to my smart jacket."

If this was his smart jacket, I was glad he wasn't wearing his gardening jacket.

"Anyway, once the coppers started going through my jacket pockets, they discovered all manner of stuff I

59

swear I'd never put there – a load of empty pill packets that were nothing to do with me."

Hector took a sip of his wine. "Must have been a quiet day at the station for them to go to such trouble over nothing. Perhaps they were bored."

"Bored or not, they took my fingerprints, and Kitty's. She didn't like that much, I can tell you."

"What did Kitty have to say?" I asked.

"Nothing, silly old fool that she is. Sees things that aren't there but misses things right under her nose. But she seemed right upset when they took me off to the station to ask more tom-fool questions. They soon brought me home, though. Couldn't pin nothing on me. All a waste of time, if you ask me."

"Weren't the police curious about Bunny's trip to the churchyard? Especially once they found out Kitty couldn't have taken her there due to her agoraphobia."

Billy drained his glass. "Kitty told them she thought it was a case of alien abduction. Away with the fairies more like. I think they think she took Bunny on some mad outing in her wheelchair in a fit of spring fever, or else they're putting it down as a domestic squabble that they don't want to get involved in. They might well be right on either of those counts. My sap's definitely rising."

I didn't want to think about that image.

"And they're always squabbling, Bunny and Kitty. Best cure would be for the cops to take 'em both away, lock 'em in a prison cell together to fight it out between 'em, and not open the door until only one of them's left alive. That'd put an end to their nonsense."

I gave a hollow laugh. "Gosh, I'm glad you're not in charge of social justice, Billy. But how is Bunny now? Have you and Kitty heard from the hospital?"

He folded his arms across his chest.

"My priority has been on saving my own bacon, not playing doctors and nurses. Which reminds me: I haven't had my tea yet."

Hector fetched a packet of Billy's favourite smoky bacon crisps from the bar and set it down in front of him. Billy started to stuff crisps in his mouth several at a time. After the first few mouthfuls, he paused and looked up.

"I will say this much for the police, though – they do make a decent cup of tea." He leaned forward and tapped the side of his nose confidentially. "Between you and me, I wonder whether they just didn't want me to say nothing in front of Kitty. In case it made her hysterical, like. They've probably got her on their files somewhere, from all the mischief she got up to in her festival days."

Billy picked up the crisp packet and tipped the last crumbs into his mouth.

"Still, I'm glad they're both all right." Billy sat back and wiped his greasy fingers on his trousers. "And I bet Kitty put the key in my pocket. She's done that before when I've left it behind by mistake, so that none of those pesky cats can chase it under the dresser out of reach. No doubt she put the pill packets in there too. It wouldn't be the first time she's used my coat as a dustbin."

As he thrust his hands into his present jacket pocket, I wondered whether he might find more surprises. To our mutual relief, he found none.

"At first I didn't see why the police were so bothered about a few empty pill packets, because Bunny and Kitty are both under the doctor for various ailments. I don't know what for exactly, and if it's women's troubles I don't want to know, neither. But then one of the policemen pointed out that the empty packets were from a legitimate prescription for Bunny, made up only a couple of days ago by the pharmacist. Carol had given it to me to deliver only the day before."

He leaned forward, clutching his beer glass to his chest. "And do you know what? They were sleeping pills. And although they were a month's supply, all the little blister packets of tablets were empty."

I gasped. "Bunny overdosed? You think she tried to kill herself?"

Billy drained his tankard. "No. Kitty looked after Bunny's pills for her. With her arthritic hands, Bunny could never get them out of the packets. When I phoned the hospital from the Manor House this afternoon, they'd just had her blood test results back. They showed an unexpected presence in her bloodstream of some kind of sedative, administered early this morning. I bet it was from the packet I'd just collected for her from the village shop."

10 Not for the Good of her Health

Billy clasped his hands on the bar-room table in front of him, like a high court judge presiding at the bench. "If they were sleeping pills, I reckon someone used them to put Kitty to sleep, then Bunny, so Kitty couldn't stop Bunny being kidnapped."

"Kidnapped?" I swallowed. "So you suspect foul play too?"

"Why, what else do you think it might be?" said Billy. "A charity outing to give her a treat?"

I sighed and turned to Hector. "I wish you'd gone to the churchyard instead of me this morning." I fixed him with an accusing look. "The doctor might have listened to you more than he did to me. I think he's a bit of a misogynist. I could have dealt with the Battersby rep's visit, you know."

Without looking at me, Hector continued to question Billy. "I think you mean abducted, Billy. In a case of kidnap, there'd be someone asking for a ransom. By the way, did Tommy bring the wheelchair back? Dr Perkins asked him to, and we saw him careering down the High Street in it."

"Yes," said Billy, "but the police didn't even bother to check it for fingerprints. They said it was too covered in sherbet powder to yield useful fingerprints."

I grimaced. "Dr Perkins did bribe Tommy with money for sweets."

"On strict instructions only to spend it after he'd delivered the wheelchair," added Hector, "but perhaps that was an unrealistic request."

"Either that or we're looking for a mad abductor with a very sweet tooth and a Sherbet Fountain habit." My forced smile quickly disappeared. "Hang on, are you sure it was sherbet? Might that have been a police euphemism?"

I'd never seen cocaine in real life, but presumed it would look much the same as the sugar crystals in a sherbet packet.

Hector looked unconvinced. "But never mind who did what for now. More importantly, did the hospital say whether Bunny is going to be OK?"

"More than likely," said Billy. "Dr Perkins phoned the Manor House after he'd spoken to the hospital. He got more sense out of them than I did. He said they're going to keep her in for a few days while the poisons clear out of her system. I'll keep an eye on Kitty in the meantime, to make sure she doesn't do anything daft."

"Well done, Bill," said Hector, sounding relieved. "With her brothers not being on the spot, it's just as well you're still close by."

Billy shuffled to the end of the bench and picked up his empty tankard to return to the bar. "Well, if you can't depend on your family, who can you trust?"

"Friends and neighbours?" said Hector gently. "By the way, I thought I might take a run up to the hospital tomorrow. Do you want to come?"

Billy shook his head. "No, I don't like hospitals," he said. "Nasty places, full of sick people." He broke into a paroxysm of coughing as he retrieved a battered pack of cigarettes from his inside jacket pocket. "But give her my regards and tell her to get well soon. I'm going out for a smoke. Then I'm off to the Manor House to see whether Kitty wants me to spend the night, in case of intruders. The woman's a bundle of nerves at the best of times."

"Just give me a shout if you need any help," I called after him. "Remember, I'm only two doors away."

We waited until he was beyond hearing distance before saying any more.

"Probably healthier for the hospital if he does stay away," said Hector. "That cough of his will be as good as any barking guard dog to frighten off housebreakers. Still, I don't think any woman should have to spend the night alone after such a traumatic day, don't you agree, Sophie?"

I nudged him reprovingly. "Now you're just using the situation to your own advantage."

"Every detective needs a sidekick." He winked at me.

"OK, then, I'll let you be mine. As long as you don't start playing the violin at unsociable hours."

"All right, I'll leave that to you," he said, sharing the last from the wine bottle between our two glasses. "Now, drink up, and then we'd better make a move, just in case Billy and Kitty need us sooner rather than later. It would be good to be within shouting distance tonight."

"You mean you're going to spend the night at my house?" That was a surprise. He'd never done so before. Although I'd slept plenty of times at his flat above the shop, staying at my house seemed taboo to him. He claimed he'd feel odd sleeping in my aunt's old bed, as he'd known her so well since he was a little boy, and she'd helped him set up the bookshop.

But I wasn't about to complain. Whoever had disrupted Kitty and Bunny's lives seemed to be oiling the wheels of mine.

11 Kitty's Catty

By the time I brought the breakfast tray upstairs, Hector was already sitting up in my bed, wide awake.

I wondered what Auntie May would have made of this development. Never mind Auntie May, it might take me some time to get used to the idea. After longing for Hector to come and stay at my cottage, now I was having second thoughts. My relationship with Damian had started to go wrong when he'd started spending nights at mine. The nights turned into weeks and months, and soon I was his financial benefactor and sponsor as much as his girlfriend.

I set the breakfast tray down carefully on Hector's lap. "Hold this tray and don't move your legs till I get back in." I climbed back up on to the old oak bedstead and slipped my legs under the duvet. "How long do you think they'll keep Bunny in for?"

Hector helped himself to a slice of buttered toast. "With any luck we'll find out today. I wonder whether we can tempt Kitty into the Land Rover to come with us?"

67

I took a sip of orange juice. "As soon as I'm dressed, I'll pop down and ask her. Worst that can happen is that she says no."

Hector hesitated with his coffee cup half way to his lips. "Are you sure you haven't put any sleeping tablets in here, Sophie? Just to keep me captive in your bed a little longer?"

I slapped him lightly on his bare chest. "That joke is in terrible taste."

He grinned. "Sorry, you're right. But I must say, I did sleep much better than I expected. Eventually." He patted the firm feather mattress with his free hand.

I looked at him archly. "I'm saying nothing," I said, before realising that made no sense whatsoever.

When Kitty opened the front door to me, the first thing that struck me was the smell of frying bacon.

A chunky tabby cat slipped past her bare feet and padded silently out to throw itself down on the flagstone path behind me.

"Tell them whatever they're selling, you don't want any," shouted a familiar voice from the kitchen. Billy. I was glad they were reconciled.

Kitty turned round to call to him over her shoulder. "It's only some girl. I'll be with you in a minute." She stood with one hand firmly on the doorknob and the other on the doorjamb, like a bouncer trying to bar my entry to a seedy nightclub. "Hello. What do you want?"

Could Kitty have forgotten who I was already, or was she just plain rude?

I spoke loudly enough so that Billy might realise it was me and come to lend moral support. "Hector and I are going to visit your mother in hospital this morning, and we wondered whether you'd like to come with us."

"Not now, we're just having breakfast – a big proper fry-up." That was the first time I'd seen her even come close to smiling. I grinned at the evidence of her sneaky return to carnivorous living in her mother's absence. I didn't want to spoil her simple pleasure.

"We can wait till you've finished your breakfast, if you like. We can go any time this morning."

"No. Let the hospital look after her for a change. I'm having a holiday while I can."

That sounded encouraging. "Oh, that's nice. Where are you going?" Perhaps her supposed agoraphobia was on the wane after all.

"Nowhere. I don't need to go anywhere. I'm just staying here and having a rest. And Billy's staying to keep me company till Mother comes home. Goodbye."

Abruptly she closed the door, leaving me staring at the peeling paint on the knocker.

"That's me told," I said to the cat, bending down to stroke its glistening fur. It looked in much better condition than Kitty as it followed me to the end of the front path, then left me to return alone to Hector.

12 The Prevention of Cats

On arrival at the hospital, we found a middle-aged lady with helmet hair camped out at Bunny's bedside. An array of goods covered the cellular blanket tucked in around the old lady's tiny frame, as if a pedlar was showing her his wares. A vast supermarket bouquet lay at the foot of the bed, alongside a wicker basket of fruit. Tucked beside a pineapple was a leaflet promoting a cat charity, and peeking out from under a bunch of grapes was a brochure about remembering the charity in a will.

This display of plenty made the bunch of grape hyacinths that I'd brought along from my back garden in a jam jar look mean.

Bunny was fast asleep, but the visitor looked up as Hector and I approached. I was wondering whether she was one of Bunny's other children, until I saw the slogan on her sweatshirt, "Cats' Prevention", and made the connection with the leaflets and gifts. Here was a woman on a mission.

"Cats Prevention?" I said aloud. "That's an odd name for a charity."

The lady gave a supercilious smile. "Our full title is Cats' Controlled Reproduction Association for the

Prevention of Strays, but one had to shorten it to fit on one's chest."

"Why didn't you just use the initials?" I asked without thinking it through.

Hector went to fetch a spare bedside chair from the other side of the ward. "I can see why not," he said quietly as he passed me, the corners of his mouth twitching.

He placed the chair on the opposite side of Bunny's bed from the Cats Prevention lady and beckoned me to sit down. He remained standing at the foot of the bed, by Bunny's medical charts. With a white coat, he'd have passed for a very dashing doctor on his rounds.

The woman's smile vanished. "I take it you're not a cat lover, sir? You're not Kitty's son, are you?"

That sobered him up.

"Good lord, no. Besides, Kitty doesn't have any children that I know of."

"Just as well, if she treats them like poor Mrs Carter's cats. Knocking them about, kicking them out of the door. Honestly, if I didn't care so much for Mrs Carter, I should have reported her daughter to the authorities long ago and got a lifetime ban on pet ownership slapped on her."

She stared at me as if looking for a family resemblance.

"And are you a relative of the Carters?"

"No, are you?" I smiled sweetly, pleased to turn the tables on her. If she had been a relative, she'd have known Kitty didn't have children.

"No," she replied quickly. "I'm just a close friend with Mrs Carter's best interests at heart."

It was an odd sort of close friendship if they weren't even on first name terms.

"I'm Mrs Petunia Lot, director of Cats Prevention. And you are—?" She narrowed her eyes at me. In a cat, that would have been a sign of friendship, but not in this case.

"Her next-door neighbour but one," I said.

"Her close neighbour," said Hector, straight faced.

"My name is Sophie Sayers," I continued. "And I work at Hector's House, just up the road from Bunny."

"Ah, so you're a cleaning lady?" She flashed a patronising smile, as if she'd put me in my place, firmly beneath her. "Do let me have your number, in case my current treasure ever decides to leave my service. A good cleaner is so hard to find these days."

"No, I sell books. Hector's House is the bookshop in Wendlebury Barrow High Street. Surely you must have seen it when you've been visiting Bunny?"

I used her first name to hint that I was on closer terms with the patient than she was, even though I wasn't.

"Bunny?"

Puzzled, she glanced at the board over the bed that bore what must have been Bunny's legal name, Christabel. I thought it very pretty.

"Mrs Carter is known to her friends and family as Bunny," said Hector.

The Cats Prevention lady ignored her gaffe as if it had never happened. "The village bookshop? Oh no, dear, I never go in there. I buy all my books online. So much cheaper, and they're delivered to your door."

At Hector's sharp intake of breath, she returned her attention to him.

"And you are?"

"I am Hector." He spoke slowly, controlling himself.

"Oh." She paused, then for no apparent reason gave a yelp of laughter that turned the heads of patients in

73

beds further down the ward. How Bunny slept through that was a miracle. She was shrill enough to wake the dead. "Oh well, never mind."

Finally, she focused on the object of her visit, turning in her chair to gaze with fake adoration at Bunny. "But what a shock this has been. Still, perhaps good will come of it yet. It's a wake-up call to the unsuitability of Mrs Carter's conditions at home. I trust the authorities will now take action to rehome her somewhere with proper care."

"But the Manor House is her home," I protested. "She's lived there for decades. And her daughter lives with her as her full-time carer."

Mrs Lot cast me a knowing look. "Quite. And her daughter can't even look after cats properly, never mind her mother."

Kitty might not have been the model cat-owner, but I couldn't imagine her tipping her mother off a kitchen chair.

Mrs Lot pressed on. "She'd be much better in a proper care home, with her own little room, than rattling around in that big house with that addled daughter of hers. Then Kitty would be free to go and get the professional help she needs for herself."

I looked to Hector to back me up, but he'd folded his arms and pursed his lips, refusing to rise to this wretched woman's endless prattle.

"Of course, I'd miss being able to depend upon her to place so many of my precious foundlings."

"You mean your cats?"

"Yes. But I'm sure Mrs Carter will continue her support in other ways."

As she spoke, she glanced at the wills leaflet tucked in beside the grapes, possibly without realising.

I followed Hector's suit and refused to engage. How Bunny left her estate was no business of Mrs Lot's, any more than it was ours, and she certainly should not be discussing it with strangers over the poor lady's sick bed.

Mrs Lot glanced at her watch.

"Are you a cat person?" she asked Hector with a saccharine smile.

"No, I'm a Mister Man," said Hector, sullenly.

After that, she ignored Hector completely.

"I like cats, if that's what you mean," I said cautiously. "My mum and dad have always had cats"

"You may care to visit the Cats Prevention headquarters in Slate Green to see our fine work for yourself." From beneath a bunch of bananas in the fruit basket, she pulled out a card showing its location map and, with a knowing smile, leaned over Bunny's legs to press it into my hand. "I defy you to leave without taking one of our lovely strays home with you!"

"Over my dead body," murmured Hector. "Or possibly yours."

If she heard him, she was unperturbed.

"Now, I must get on. I've two more elderly friends to see here this morning before getting back for our open afternoon at the refuge. See you again, no doubt, Chloe Mayer."

With a smug smile, as if she thought she'd just made a new conquest, she scooped up her handbag from the floor, and bent over the bed to air-kiss Bunny somewhere near her left cheekbone. Then she patted the hand without the cannula for the drip before bustling off towards the exit without a backward glance, probably already planning her attack on the next patient on her hit list.

13 Sleeping Beauty

A new voice broke the welcome silence that followed Mrs Lot's departure.

"Good riddance." Bunny's eyes snapped open as soon as the double swing doors at the end of the ward closed behind her. "Wretched woman, I thought she'd never leave. Littering my bed with her bribes." From beneath the thin hospital blanket, Bunny kicked the supermarket shopping strewn at the foot of her bed.

"I'll give the sweets to the nurses, but you can take the rest of it back for Kitty. That'll make sure she eats something healthy in my absence. And give the flowers to Carol to sell in her shop. Honestly, that wretched cat woman comes to my house every week without invitation and seems to think she's doing me a favour. I hoped I'd have a break from her in here. She's only after my money, you know. Even thinks she's in with a chance of inheriting my house. Still, at least having her about the place keeps Kitty on her toes. As do all the cats."

She laughed, and Hector let out a sigh of relief.

"Hello, Bunny, I'm glad to see you're feeling better. We thought you were out for the count when we got here."

"Just playing dead for Mrs Peculiar Lot's benefit. Ha! Lot's wife. I wish someone would turn her into a pillar of salt."

She savoured that thought before turning her silver-grey eyes on me. With a starburst of wrinkles at the outer corners, her eyes were bright and lively above her distinctive aquiline nose and wide, thin-lipped mouth.

"So you're Sophie Sayers. Hello, my dear."

Age may have softened the angles familiar from Kitty's face, but Bunny retained the poise and confidence of someone used to having her exquisite high cheekbones admired. I liked her already.

"Yes, that's right, Mrs Carter. I'm Sophie Sayers, and I live two doors up from you. I'm sorry I've never got round to visiting you before now. At home, I mean."

"And I'm sorry I've never thought to invite you, so now we're quits. But please call me Bunny. All my friends do. Hector, next time you bring my books, you must bring Sophie too. She looks interesting."

Hector glanced from her to me and back again. "If you like," he said with a reluctance that surprised me. Perhaps he enjoyed his time alone with her. It seemed ridiculous to feel jealous of such an elderly lady, but I envied her easy charm. I hastened to change the subject.

"Anyway, how are you feeling now after your ordeal?"

With fingers swan-necked from arthritis, she pulled back the drooping sleeves of her hospital gown to reveal arms so covered in dark bruises that there was hardly a patch of flesh-coloured flesh to be seen.

"Black and blue," she said tersely. "And in pain." She pointed to the cannula in the back of her hand. "They've put me on fluids and painkillers to help me bear it, but they're not keen to give me any more drugs than they have to. One of the nurses said they didn't want to overtax my liver. I can think of better ways to overtax my liver." She glanced disparagingly at the bottle of lemon barley water on her bedside cabinet then gazed imploringly at Hector. "I don't suppose you've got any of your lovely hooch on you, dearie?"

He patted his jacket pockets, pretending to check. "No, sorry. I'll sneak you some later when you're back at home, if you like." I guessed he meant to sneak it past Kitty. "But tell me, do you feel as if you're on the mend? Despite the bruises, you seem on good form."

She was certainly chirpier than one might expect, considering what she'd been through.

"Oh, I'll pass muster. I'll be here for a few days, till they unhitch me from this wretched thing." She tugged at the tube hard enough to make the drip stand rattle. "I dare say they'll send me home as soon as they can get away with it, to clear the bed for some needier soul."

"You're not worried about going home?" I was fearful on her behalf. Who was to say her attacker wouldn't strike again?

"Worried? Why should I be worried?"

Hector flashed me a restraining look, so I let him reply. He paused to gather the right words.

"Bunny, do you remember your accident?"

She waved a hand dismissively. "Tumbling down a rabbit hole like Alice? Mercy, yes! Well, I remember waking up in it, if not falling down."

"Do you have any recollection how you got there?"

She threw up her hands in surrender. "No idea. Perhaps I was sleepwalking. Those sleeping pills are very good, you know. I'm just glad I slept through the whole thing until Dr Perkins woke me up. Best sleep I've had in ages, though the bruises are a high price to pay."

She gazed down at her purple wrists.

"The thing is, no-one seems to know how you got there."

She pursed her lips. "No matter. If anyone tries any funny business, Kitty will stop them."

"Kitty didn't stop them this time," he said gently. "Your wheelchair was found abandoned in the churchyard. Do you remember anyone visiting you yesterday and taking you out in your wheelchair? Kitty doesn't."

"Kitty wouldn't remember her own name if I didn't call her by it." She leaned back against her pillows, wincing slightly at the effort. "Now, let me see. Billy came to do the gardening – no, that was the previous day. Was it Dr Perkins? I distinctly remember seeing Dr Perkins."

"No, that was later," I said. "I called him to attend to you in the churchyard after your fall."

"And I certainly don't remember going out in my wheelchair. I haven't touched it for months. Whoever it was might have carted me down there in a wheelbarrow, for all I know."

Stiffly Bunny turned her head to one side to make herself more comfortable, showing off her remarkable profile to best advantage. Waves of hair spread out on the pillow behind her like spun silver. For the first time she noticed my little jam jar of grape hyacinths that I'd set on her bedside locker when we arrived. She reached out to touch them.

"Beautiful," she said, half-closing her eyes like a cat in bliss. Hector, still at the foot of her bed, glanced down at Petunia Lot's lavish bouquet, then back to my flowers.

"Do you know who you remind me of right now, Bunny? No, don't move. Dame Ellen Terry, in the Watts portrait, *Choosing*, though in reverse."

"Ah!" said Bunny, raising a hand and cupping it around the hyacinths.

Hector turned to me. "Do you know it, Sophie? A famous Victorian painting showing a beautiful woman choosing between the humble but exquisitely perfumed violets in her hand, and showy unscented hothouse camellias at her shoulder."

Then he reached into his inside jacket pocket.

"Which reminds me, Bunny, I've brought you a small volume of poetry to divert you. It's hard to concentrate on a novel in the hubbub of a hospital, especially if you're feeling below par, but I thought these poems might offer some respite."

He presented her with a small vintage hardback with a dark green binding. It must have come from his private collection of second-hand books rather than from the shop. She took it with both hands and tilted the spine towards her at arm's length to focus on the title.

"Ah, John Clare." She smiled, set it down and patted its cover. "Bless you, Hector." When she reached out to press Hector's hand, her smile was reflected by his.

Then she dropped his hand abruptly, picked up the book, opened it at the first page and began to read. After turning to the next page, she glanced up as if surprised to see us still there.

"Thank you for coming," she said, which was possibly the politest way she could think of to tell us to go.

14 Priti in Pink

Leaving Bunny engrossed in the book, and taking with us most of the gifts that Mrs Lot had brought, we headed for the nurses' station. A lady in a pink dress with Priti on her name badge looked up from her paperwork to greet us.

"How can I help you?"

Hector flashed her his best smile, the one I wished he kept reserved for me.

"Thank you so much, nurse. We'd be most grateful for an update on my great aunt, Christabel Carter. I promised to get an update for her daughter, who lives with her. Can you offer me any insights about her current condition and her prognosis so that we may prepare appropriately for her return? That would be most kind of you."

He was rather overdoing the charm.

"Of course, sir." She got up to fetch Bunny's file from a stack of trays. "Ah yes, Mrs Carter." Flipping it open, she ran a slender forefinger down a page of doctor's scrawl, then turned the page to inspect some lab reports, before looking up into Hector's still-smiling eyes.

"It looks as if she'll be here for a few more days yet, until the sedatives have left her system. We also need to be sure the bruising has stopped coming out, and we'll run another liver function test before her release. Do you think she'd taken too many of her prescription sleeping pills by mistake?"

Hector shook his head. "Her daughter, my cousin, manages her medication, so it seems unlikely."

The nurse leaned forward. "Might it have been something she bought over the internet?" She lowered her voice. "She wouldn't be the first elderly patient to self-medicate inappropriately from an online order. Usually it's the gentlemen, if you know what I mean."

She winked at Hector, and he grinned back, complicit in her suggestiveness.

Turning my back on their shameless flirting, I went to fetch a paper cup of water from the dispenser in the waiting area, drinking it quickly to resist the temptation to throw it over the pair of them. Then I sat down in an armchair and picked up a trashy magazine from the coffee table. I'd just started reading an interesting article about a woman who had married her grandson's best friend when Hector strolled over, grabbed my hand and pulled me to my feet.

"Home time, sweetheart."

He marched us quickly through the ward's swing doors and down the corridor towards the exit. Only when we were out of earshot did he deign to speak.

"I think I got away with it. It sounds as if whatever knocked Bunny out, it wasn't her own prescription drugs that were in Billy's pocket. Billy didn't have a hand in this. Those empty packets must have been a plant." Anger was rising in his voice as he spoke.

I stopped and stared at him. "Unless there's a chance that she was trying to kill herself?"

He shook his head. "Did you ever see an old lady with less intention of going to her grave? She's positively sprinting to keep ahead of time's winged chariot. No, someone's up to no good here. I just hope to God it wasn't Kitty. Billy thinks Kitty was drugged too, which is why he couldn't wake her before the ambulance took Bunny away. But who would have drugged them both, and how, and why?"

We started down the stairs towards the main entrance.

"Though I hate to suggest it, I suppose there's a chance that Kitty drugged Bunny first, hoping to polish her off, then, filled with remorse, took an overdose herself," said Hector.

"No, Kitty was only unconscious for a little while. And she bounced back soon enough with little more than a hangover. I didn't catch whether the nurse said the hospital had reported it to the police."

"No. It seems the hospital put it down to patient error, despite the strange circumstances in which Bunny was found. Especially as the ambulance was called by a member of the medical profession. Fellow medics stick together as a rule."

I remembered Billy's resentment of the doctor's leisure. "Ex-medic."

"Once a doctor, always a doctor. Even so, it does seem odd that Dr Perkins didn't call the police." He held the fire door open to let me pass through to the entrance lobby.

"Perhaps, like Billy, he assumed it was just the result of a row between mother and daughter, and he wanted to protect Kitty from prosecution. He must feel some allegiance to them as longstanding patients of his."

"Probably. Besides, if a doctor suspected Kitty of attempted murder, not to call the police would count as professional misconduct, or even criminal negligence. It could be enough to get him struck off the medical register."

Leaving the building via the revolving door, we headed towards the visitor car park.

"Now he's retired, being struck off might not bother him."

Hector stopped to look at me. "If someone's spent their whole career doing a professional job, that will be a huge part of who they are, even in retirement. He wouldn't want to be 'Othello, with his occupation gone'. A defrocked priest. A cabbie without a driving licence. But I agree, there's something odd here. And I don't get it."

Reaching the ticket machine, Hector punched in his vehicle registration and tapped his debit card against the contactless card reader before continuing.

"I can see an old person might make a mistake with their own prescription, forgetting they'd taken a tablet and accidentally popping a second. I've done that with antibiotics before now. But not enough to knock themselves out, before following it up with a solo outing to a graveyard in fancy dress."

"Well, if the police aren't taking an interest, all the more reason for us to, in case there's more mischief yet to come." I hesitated. "By the way, I didn't know you were related to Bunny, until I heard you telling the nurse that she was your aunt. I know half the village is related to each other, but I didn't know you were part of her family."

I was miffed that he had told an attractive stranger in a nurse's uniform something about himself that I didn't know.

Hector slipped the key into the door of his Land Rover. "She isn't really my aunt, silly. I was just saying that to get the nurse to tell me Bunny's prognosis." Was he telling the truth now? "So who do you think is behind it?"

I grinned. "If it's motive you're after, my money's on that cat lady. Such extravagant gifts! Talk about transparent!"

Hector shook his head in disbelief at her gall. "On the other hand, maybe one or all of Bunny's children are impatient for their inheritance and are trying to hasten nature's course? Perhaps they have money problems?" I shuddered. "I know that's a horrible thought, but I can't think of any other reason someone might want to murder her."

"A jealous lover?" I said, half in jest, as I climbed up into the passenger seat. "She's still got charisma, despite her old age."

Hector stopped in the middle of fastening his seat belt and stared at me. "Goodness, is that your preferred method for ending a relationship? I'd better watch my back."

15 Inspector Murray of the Churchyard

After we'd parked the Land Rover back at the shop, I persuaded Hector that we should revisit the scene of the crime – for that was what I was now convinced it was – to uncover any clues that we'd missed the previous morning.

"Wouldn't it be wonderful to find that the police had changed their minds, decided to investigate, and cordoned the churchyard off with that special police tape you see on telly, saying 'Crime Scene, Do Not Enter'?"

"I'm afraid it's about as likely as discovering a Bunny-shaped chalk outline at the bottom of the grave."

To my disappointment, the only uniformed man we met as we passed through the lychgate was wearing not blue, but black. The Reverend Murray, in full robes for morning service, was standing alone at the foot of the now empty grave, shoulders hunched in quiet contemplation. Someone had spread the artificial grass to cover the open grave again and secured it with a couple of very long logs. At our approach, the vicar looked up forlornly. This episode must have upset him too.

I hoped our good news from the hospital might cheer him up. "We've just been to visit Bunny, and she's on good form."

"I wondered why you weren't in church," he said. I hadn't previously gone to the Sunday service, but given my imminent role as Sunday School teacher, it was something I should have started doing by now. However, nothing had been further from my thoughts when I'd woken up in bed with Hector that morning.

But the vicar wasn't about to scold me. He was too preoccupied with thoughts of the grave. "Poor Bunny. This dreadful business has put me in a quandary about Mr Harper's funeral too."

"Who is Mr Harper?" I asked.

"The rightful owner of this grave. He chose and paid for the plot years ago and died just last week. Now I don't know whether to go ahead and use it for his burial, or to start afresh elsewhere. I wouldn't want his family to feel their father's grave has been tainted with scandal. The only acceptable time to reuse a grave is if it's been intended for another occupant all along."

I grimaced. "That sounds ghoulish."

The vicar raised his eyebrows. "Not at all, my dear. It's common practice for married couples to buy a joint plot, with the second to die buried on top of the first. Such graves are dug a little deeper, of course, so that the second coffin will still be the regulation depth beneath the surface. This one is a single. Mrs Harper was cremated and her ashes scattered in the woods at bluebell time last year."

Scanning the churchyard for joint graves, I spotted one in which the second occupant had been added less than a year after the first.

"I suppose Bunny's grave's already sorted, if she had three dead husbands go before her?" said Hector. "She'll be spoiled for choice."

The vicar shook his head. "Funnily enough, one of her sons phoned to ask me that a week or two ago. I can't remember now whether it was Stuart or Paul. They both sound the same on the phone. I had to look back through the parish records to find out. It turned out each of her three husbands had a single plot. Perhaps when she buried the third, she hadn't planned for him to be her last."

"He may not be yet," I said. "You never know, her recent accident may incline her to seize the day and marry again for one last chance of happiness."

The vicar sighed. "What it is to be young and romantic."

"Did you have any candidates in mind for her, Sophie?" asked Hector, squeezing my hand. "Let's hope it's not to some gold-digger marrying her for her money."

"Not yet, but if I come across any, I'll run them past you for approval."

"Dear me, this is no way to talk of the blessed sacrament of marriage," said the vicar, although he was smiling. I was glad we had lifted him out of his despondency. He turned his back on it to give us his full attention.

Hector steered the conversation back to our investigation. "It must be unusual to bury three husbands in the same churchyard, Vicar, although convenient."

I squinted against the sunshine to read more inscriptions. "Where exactly are Bunny's husbands' graves?"

Hector nudged me. "Now who's being ghoulish?"

"Follow me." The vicar led us to one of the newer, shinier headstones, a black slab dotted with tiny sparkles. The fragments of some kind of ore reminded me of the glitter on a Christmas card. "Here's her most recent husband, Joss Carter."

"'My Last Duchess'," murmured Hector.

"Robert Browning," I replied, pleased to remember that poem from my English GCSE studies.

Colonising the ground in front of the headstone was a mass of lily-of-the-valley shoots, not yet in bud, but with the promise of their delicate fragrance yet to come. They must have been planted years ago and left to naturalise, like the cluster in my garden under Auntie May's apple tree – a practical alternative to returning with fresh flowers each week, and the sign of a mourner who had moved on.

As the vicar led us towards the back of the churchyard, I wondered where my grave would be. And Hector's. If we were buried together, which one of us would be on top? Which would I prefer? I remembered Billy's poem: "The grave's a fine and private place, but none, I think, do there embrace." It probably wouldn't matter either way.

"Here's old Lucas Brady," the vicar was saying. "He was her second husband." The surface was dotted with tiny cyclamen. Then he passed down to an earlier row. "And there's Mungo Jenkins, her first." His grave bore only grass.

"How lovely that Mr Brady's grave's got fresh flowers on it too."

"They must be from one of his sons," said the vicar. "They pay the occasional flying visit to the Manor House. Funnily enough, Paul called in at the vicarage only yesterday to offer to repair my faulty guttering – or was it Stuart? No, it was definitely Paul. Stuart's the accountant, Paul's the builder. Stuart for sums, Paul plumbs, that's how I remember which is which. Apparently, Paul's just started doing a bit of work for Donald at The Bluebird, and Donald told him my guttering needed fixing. But Paul wouldn't take any payment from me. Very kind of him."

He bent down to peer at the plastic flower wrapper. "Yes, fuel-station flowers. Most likely from the garage between here and Slate Green. A token tribute from a man in a hurry. Still, well intended, I'm sure." As he straightened his back, I caught the forgiving twinkle in his eye.

"What about her other seven children?" I asked. "Do they ever come back to Wendlebury?"

"Those were all from her first marriage. Jenkinses, every one of them. All took umbrage when she remarried, and I'm not sure she hears from any of those who are still alive, except perhaps at Christmas. They all left the parish long before I took up my post here, so I don't know any of them personally."

"Strange to have so many children from the first marriage, but only two from the second and one from the third," I said thoughtfully. "I wonder what happened?"

"They call it the Pill," said Hector. "You may have heard of it, Sophie."

The vicar looked away to spare my blushes, but I could see his shoulders shaking in silent laughter as he turned his back.

Feeling sorry for Mungo Jenkins, alone with neither wife nor offspring, I went over to pull a few stray weeds out of his plot. As senior husband, he deserved better. While Hector and the vicar chatted in tones too low for me to hear, I plucked a handful of early daisies from the surrounding grass and made them into a chain as long as my arm, carefully splitting each furry stalk with my thumbnail. Once I'd laid it carefully along the top of Mungo's headstone, I felt better.

Then I went to visit Auntie May, her spot now resplendent with the branches of cherry blossom I'd brought from her garden after work the day before. I knew the flowers wouldn't last long away from the tree. The petals were already starting to blow like confetti in the slight midday breeze.

I smiled. She'd have liked that. She had enjoyed several trips to Japan to write about cherry blossom.

The vicar took his leave. "Sunday dinner time," he called across to me cheerfully. "Mustn't be late for my dear wife."

He'd probably already booked their joint plot.

Hector strolled over to admire May's new headstone and gave it an affectionate pat.

"Fancy lunch at The Bluebird?" He checked his watch. "It'll give us strength to go and report to Kitty on our hospital visit."

I suspected Hector was just trying to put off returning to the Manor House, but when we arrived at the pub, I discovered he had other plans.

16 Courting Paul

Instead of heading for our usual booth, Hector strode up to the bar. Settling on a stool, he leaned forward on the counter, flashing a big, open smile at Donald, who was busy replenishing a basket with packets of mixed nuts from a cardboard box. I perched on the stool beside him.

"Afternoon, you two. What are you both looking so cheerful about?" He rolled his eyes. "All right for some, able to lie about in bed all morning."

Hector tried to look more serious. "Actually, we were up with the lark, doing our social duty. We've just been to see Bunny Carter in hospital."

Donald folded the empty cardboard carton down flat and tucked it under the counter. "Was her son Paul there? He said he'd be paying her a visit today."

"I wouldn't know him if I saw him," I said.

"You can't miss him. He looks just like Kitty, only thinner, taller, balder and less addled. Much thinner than he used to be, come to think of it. Anyone would think his wife doesn't feed him. Mind you, he was eating heartily enough when he was in here last night, so it's not for lack of appetite. Maybe they've split up."

I pursed my lips and waved an admonishing finger at him. "Donald! That's how rumours start!"

He grinned. "Only joking. We were glad to have his custom. Enthusiastic eaters are always welcome in our restaurant."

"The vicar was just telling us Paul had also called in to see him yesterday," said Hector.

"About Bunny?"

"About the vicarage guttering. He offered to fix it for free."

"That's good of him," said Donald. "I did drop Paul a little hint. Nice of him to follow it up. And he's given me an excellent price for the next round of building work in my courtyard. I've told him he can start tomorrow if he's got the manpower available."

A middle-aged man in gardening clothes, seated further along the bar, got up to shift his stool closer to us. Donald and Hector seemed to know him, though I didn't. He leaned over confidentially. "Brady's just currying favour, if you ask me." He tapped the side of his nose. "He's trying to get people on side for when he's in a position to apply for planning permission to convert the Manor House into a care home. There's no guarantee he'll get it without effective lobbying and local support."

"He's rather counting his chickens, isn't he?" said Hector. "What makes him think it's his to plan for? Bunny told me she's keeping the terms of her will a secret."

Donald set our usual drinks in front of us.

"Can you start a tab for us, please?" said Hector. "We're staying for lunch."

"Will do," said Donald, scribbling on his pad.

Hector watched the head on his beer settle. "But I can see why he's so keen. If he did it up like his other care homes, it would add value to the property and provide a good income. In its current state, it's just a money pit. It needs loads of work done to the fabric of the building just to bring it back into good repair. Bunny and Kitty will never be able to fund any work like that."

"It's a bit of an eyesore for the village, crumbling about their ears," said Donald. "I say good luck to him."

"See what I mean?" grumbled the gardener. "Brady's got you on side already. He's a sly bugger, that one."

Donald frowned. "He was certainly doing his best to win over Billy last night."

"Billy?" I set down my glass of wine so suddenly that a little slopped over the edge on to the bar towel. "I thought Billy was staying the night at Kitty's to keep her company."

Donald glanced at me apologetically. "He just slipped out for a quick pint while she was watching her favourite game show on the telly. Bunny doesn't keep any alcohol in the house, or else Kitty would drink it. I heard that at her worst, Bunny even had to hide her perfume, or she'd down that too."

"Really?" asked Hector. "God, Donald, you're a worse gossip than any woman I know."

I slapped his thigh in admonishment and tried to steer the conversation back on track. "So did Billy just have the one pint and go back to Kitty's?"

Donald poured himself half a pint of lemonade and took a swig. "Not by the time Paul had finished with him. Throwing his money about in the bar, he was. He's got his mother's charm, persuading even those who didn't know him to accept his generosity."

"So you did well out of it," said the gardener, tersely. "Double whammy. Happy customers, happy landlord – and more on side for his plans for the Manor House.

Donald, he's got you in his pocket, my son. You'd better look out."

Donald scowled. "Are you saying I'm easily bought?" He whisked away the gardener's glass and tipped it upside down in the glass-washing sink. The gardener gazed at his empty hand, fingers still curved as if nursing the glass. Then without a word, he climbed down from the stool.

As he reached the front door, it swung open to admit a tall, lean man with sparse dark hair and the unmistakeable aquiline nose of Bunny Carter.

"Good afternoon, Mr Brady," said the gardener, his voice obsequious. "Fancy seeing you here again. That's the second time this year. This must be our lucky weekend."

For a moment, a shadow crossed Paul's face, before an ingratiating smile took over. "Good afternoon to you too, my friend. Glorious day out there."

It wasn't particularly.

"Afternoon, Paul," said Donald cheerily, as the new arrival came over to install himself on the recently vacated barstool beside us. "How's your mother?"

"What? Oh, fine, fine, thanks."

"Have you been to see her?" asked Hector politely. "Donald told us that was your plan. We've just come from the hospital ourselves. We must have missed you."

Paul stared at him analytically.

"And you are?"

"Hector Munro, of Hector's House. Your mother's one of my best customers. And this is my partner, Sophie Sayers."

Paul swivelled sharply towards me, offering me, but not Hector, his hand to shake. "May Sayers's granddaughter? You're in her cottage now?"

"Great-niece. And it's my cottage now."

Paul pointed to a beer tap to signal to Donald for a pint.

"Same again for these two, while you're at it, Don." No-one ever called Donald "Don".

Paul turned back to me. "So what sort of price would you be looking for to sell your little cottage? I'd be willing to match your top offer, so you might as well save yourself time and give me first refusal. I've had my eye on that place for a while, as well as old Hampton's next door." Out of his back pocket he pulled a business card for his property development company. "They'd make great staff accommodation for when I convert the Manor House into a care home."

I bridled. "I'm not selling. I've only just moved in, and I've no intention of living anywhere else."

He took a long gulp of beer. "A young thing like you? I can't see there's much to hold you in a sleepy place like this. Especially if you're going to have a houseful of the elderly as your neighbours."

"I happen to like old people."

Donald tried to lighten the mood. "Shall I take your orders for dinner, folks? We've beef, chicken, lamb or nut roast."

"Beef, please, Donald," said Hector, glaring at Paul.

"Nut roast for me, thanks, Donald," I said, placing my hand over Hector's, which was on my thigh. "Besides which, Joshua Hampton has no intention of moving either. That's the only house he's lived in all his life, and he's not going anywhere else."

"Really?" Paul looked away as he drank some more beer. "How old is he again? He must be older than my mother. Surely he must be starting to lose his faculties by now. Don't you worry about him inadvertently setting his house on fire, or leaving his taps running and flooding you both, or starting to behave a little oddly towards you?"

He leaned across, breathing beer in my face.

"You must know there comes a time when old people aren't capable of living on their own. Think of your own safety. I'm sure we could reserve one of our nice new rooms for him. He'd only be moving next door. He'd hardly notice the difference."

I jumped down from my stool, turning my back to Paul so he couldn't see the angry tears welling up. "Come on, Hector, let's find a table for two, shall we?"

We left untouched the drinks Paul had bought us.

"I'll bring you a bottle of your usual," Donald called after me. "It's on the house, Sophie."

"I don't know what's rattled her cage," said Paul to Donald, loudly enough for me to hear from our booth. "Surely she's bright enough to see I have my mother's best interests at heart? You'd think anyone who has seen Mother's living conditions would be glad she has at least one sensible child willing to come to her rescue."

I couldn't hear Donald's reply.

17 Consoling Kitty

"Now her gate latch is stuck. Do you think she is trying to deter visitors, or has someone been tampering with it?"

Gently Hector pushed my fumbling hands away from Kitty's front gate and opened it himself. With my arm through his, we strolled up the path towards the porch.

"Should we tell Kitty what Paul said?" I didn't want to upset Kitty, but I felt she had a right to know about his selfish intentions.

"Probably best not to risk stirring things up. He'll tell her himself if he wants to. Or perhaps she already knows. She might even be in cahoots with him. It's none of our business."

"It is my business if he's trying to evict me from my cottage. And Joshua too."

"That's slightly overstating the case, sweetheart. He has no power to evict you. The house is yours. The worst he can do is make you an offer you can't refuse. Financially speaking, I mean."

As we reached the porch, I dropped his arm to clasp my hands over my heart. "Auntie May's house is priceless."

"Well, then, you're safe. Now, let's concentrate on what we came here to do: to give Kitty news of Bunny."

He raised the door knocker, but before he could use it, the door creaked open, though there was no-one behind it to greet us. Hector stepped gingerly inside. "Hello? Kitty? Billy? It's Sophie and Hector. Can we come in? Anybody home?"

The only answer was a loud grunting snore from the direction of the kitchen, from which wafted surprisingly delicious aromas suggestive of an imminent roast beef dinner, and the faint rattling of lids on bubbling saucepans of vegetables on the Aga. Hector and I exchanged quizzical glances.

"It seems an odd time to fall asleep, right in the middle of preparing dinner," I whispered. We tiptoed down the corridor to the kitchen to investigate.

In the armchair in front of the Aga lolled Billy, head back, stockinged feet on the towel rail. Two large cats that may have once been white were curled up on his lap, equally out for the count. He had one hand resting companionably on the back of each of them, as if stroking them had sent them all off to sleep. There was no sign of Kitty.

"My goodness, Hector, do you think she's drugged him and run?"

Hector stepped forward to put his face closer to Billy's than I would have dared and sniffed his breath.

"No, I don't think so." As he straightened up, Kitty clattered in through the back door, a battered wicker basket of fresh herbs in one hand and a huge pair of rusty scissors in the other. She pulled a stained tea-towel from beneath Billy's feet and draped it over the basket.

"Mint for the sauce," she said. "Want to keep it fresh till the joint's cooked."

Hector glanced at his watch. "Sorry, Kitty, we didn't mean to interrupt your lunch. You're eating late, aren't you? We've already had ours at The Bluebird."

Kitty tossed the scissors carelessly on to the kitchen table, perilously close to a ball of black fur that immediately unfurled itself to form a three-legged one-eyed cat. It jumped down from the table and fled through the kitchen door with surprising grace for a triped. It tried to give Kitty a wide berth, but she still managed to help it on its way with the toe of her rubber gardening clog.

"I wasn't inviting you." She wiped her grass-stained hands down her garish patchwork batik skirt. "I'm sick of freeloaders."

"We've just come to tell you how your mother is," said Hector. "We've been to visit her in hospital this morning."

"Oh really? I got Billy to phone the hospital for an update this morning, but he didn't get much sense out of them. I don't like phones."

"Probably Chinese whispers," said Hector with a smile. "He's not great on the phone even with his hearing aids. But we can assure you that she's fine and in good spirits."

Kitty let out a huge sigh. She must have been more anxious than she was letting on.

"She's likely to be in hospital for a few days more for observation," Hector continued, "at least until all the poison is out of her system."

As he said the word poison, Hector watched Kitty closely for her reaction. She jumped.

"Poison? She's been poisoned? What with, rat poison?" She looked away, shaking her head. Tears had sprung into her wide, red-rimmed eyes. "That can't be right. She won't have rat poison in the house, lest her precious cats get at it."

"Not that sort of poison," said Hector. "Prescription drugs, wrongly used. She'd ingested a large dose of something that hadn't been prescribed for her."

Kitty puffed out another loud breath, this time more of exasperation, and put her hands on her hips. "What's she been doing now? I'm the one that sorts out her pills for her. I make sure she gets enough of the right ones and no more. I wouldn't make a mistake like that."

She pulled a mug off the draining board and upended an old stone teapot into it, the tea as dark as the pot. As she reached across for the milk bottle on the counter, her hand alighted on a bottle of washing-up liquid which, without looking, she squirted into her mug. As she raised her tea to her lips, Hector and I held our breath.

Just then, a pan of potatoes on the Aga began to splutter and boil over, spattering Billy's toes. He snorted in his sleep as Kitty set her mug down and shifted the pan to one side. Returning to the counter, she pulled down a couple more mugs.

"I suppose you'll want a cup of tea now you've seen me drinking mine? I can put more water in the pot if absolutely necessary."

"Oh no, please don't go to any trouble," I said. "A glass of water would be fine."

There wasn't much damage she could do to a glass of water.

"Actually a glass of water would be more trouble," she muttered, taking two tumblers to a huge ancient fridge in the corner and reaching into its icebox. She pulled out a black rubber mould full of ice and flexed it over the tumblers. Some cubes fell into the glasses, others skidded across the tiled floor. She topped up the glasses from the tap before slamming them down on the kitchen table.

"So Mother's going to be all right?" she asked.

Hector watched the ice cubes in his tumbler cracking and clicking madly against each other. She'd used the hot tap.

He looked up and gave a reassuring smile. "She'll be fine, Kitty. She was sitting up and chatting away, just like her old self. We left her enjoying a good book."

Kitty's eyes narrowed. "Did you see any other visitors?"

Hector hesitated. "Just some woman from one of the animal charities your mother supports."

Kitty cast an angry glance at the cats on Billy's lap. "Not that pesky Mrs Lot? I wouldn't put it past her to poison my mother. She reminds me of the witch in *Sleeping Beauty*." I thought of the shiny red apples in Mrs Lot's gift basket of fruit. "Always sucking up to her. Wretched cats' home! God knows, she's been getting enough dosh out of Mother even before she's dead. She'll be lucky if Mother has anything left to leave to anyone after feeding all these waifs and strays that get dumped on us."

She waved a hand towards a muddled array of cat dishes on the floor, bits of dried meat clinging to the rims, and a large aluminium dog bowl with barely a teaspoon of water puddled at the bottom. Then she glanced back at the stove.

"The potatoes are done. You'll have to go now. I need to wake Billy up to eat."

She shook him by the shoulders as she shouted his name close to his ears. "BILLY!"

105

I was starting to feel drowsy myself, my breathing falling into the same rhythm as Billy's snores. Perhaps his wasn't a natural sleep after all?

Then he opened his eyes and took a moment to register where he was and who he was with. "Afternoon, girlie. Afternoon, Hector. Kitty."

Though he was cogent, by now I was feeling very odd myself. I leaned heavily against Hector. "Come on, Hector, let's not keep Billy from his lunch. Thanks for the water, Kitty." But Kitty had already turned her back to us and was busy draining the potatoes in a dented colander over the sink.

Billy got up from the armchair, yawning and stretching, causing the cats to tumble from his lap like Jenga blocks. Then he sat down again at the messy kitchen table and grabbed a knife and fork from a basket of mismatched cutlery.

We knew when we weren't wanted. As we closed the front door behind us, I looped my hand through Hector's arm.

"I'm feeling a little pecu – pelu – odd." The porch began to spin around me. "I think there was something in that water."

"What, besides ice?"

"We only have Kitty's word that it was ice. You could freeze anything inside an ice cube. I've seen it done at parties. Cherries. Lemons. Things."

"The ice cubes looked all right to me," said Hector, putting his arm round me to prop me up.

I shook my head, then wished I hadn't. It was like being on the waltzers at the Village Show. "Something clear but deadly. Rat poison? Is that what rat poison looks like?" I clutched my stomach.

By now we'd reached my gate, and Hector opened it and guided me through.

"Must lie down." I pulled my front door key out of my pocket and thrust it towards him. "Here. You. Open."

Then everything went blank.

18 How Rumours Start

Next thing I knew, I was lying on my bed with the duvet pulled over my chest. Throwing it back, I discovered I was fully clothed.

"What the—?"

Hector looked up calmly from the window seat, where he was sitting with his feet up, reading a book.

"Let's hope none of the neighbours saw me carrying you over the threshold, or it'll be all over the village that we've just got married."

I hauled myself up and shuffled my bottom back till I was leaning against the headboard. The late afternoon sunshine streamed in through the bedroom window, and I covered my eyes with my hands. "Ooh, my head!"

The details of our visit to Kitty started to come back to me. "Where's the doctor? What does the doctor say?"

"What doctor?"

"You didn't call a doctor? If Kitty's poisoned me, that means she was probably the one who drugged Bunny. And maybe Billy too. Shall we go back and rescue him?" I squinted at Hector suspiciously. "You seem all right. Did you not drink your water?"

Hector put his book down and came to sit on the bed beside me. When he reached up to stroke a stray strand of hair away from my face, I was glad of the shadow he cast over me.

"There's nothing wrong with you or Billy that needs medical intervention. Nor with Kitty's ice cubes. You both just need to take more water with it."

"What, with the poison?"

"With the booze. I've no idea how many pints Paul poured into Billy last night, but he was still reeking of beer while we were at Kitty's. I think he was just sleeping off a hangover. Whereas you polished off a whole bottle of wine by yourself over our lunch at The Bluebird. I was holding back, in case we wanted to drive anywhere this afternoon. So when Donald gave us that bottle of wine on the house, you drank practically the whole thing by yourself."

My cheeks turned as red as the wine. "It's Paul's fault for making me so cross."

Hector smiled. "Maybe. Are you feeling better for your little sleep?"

"I suppose so. But I still think Kitty was behaving oddly."

Hector slipped off his shoes and stretched out on the bed beside me. "Kitty is odd. That's Kitty for you. But she was no odder than usual." I snuggled up to him for comfort. "I suppose she's enjoying her freedom with Bunny not being there to boss her about. But I didn't spot anything out of the ordinary."

He was just about to kiss me when I pushed him away and sat bolt upright.

"Oh, but it was. She was. Think back, now, Hector. Where was Kitty when we arrived at the Manor House this afternoon? In the kitchen?"

110

"No," he said slowly, folding his hands across his chest.

"In the garden, gathering mint for a sauce."

Hector shrugged. "So what? Mint sauce may be meant for lamb rather than beef, but I've got a friend who has apple sauce with gammon. That's not sinister, just sickly."

I shook my head. "I'm not talking about her culinary methods. I mean, she put washing-up liquid in her tea."

"Now that is an acquired taste."

"What I mean is, she was outside in the garden. She'd sneaked outside while Billy was asleep. Though she'd have everyone believe she's agoraphobic."

Hector sat up straighter. "The cheek of it! She told me she'd not been out of the house for five years. That's why I've been delivering her and Bunny's book orders all this time. She's been taking advantage of my good nature!"

"Not only that." I jabbed him in the chest with my forefinger. "If she's not really agoraphobic, it could have been her who pushed Bunny in the wheelchair up the High Street and left her for dead in Mr Harper's grave."

19 Eyes and Ears

"Have you seen my ears, Sophie?"

Jemima swung her school book bag on to my small teaching desk in the stockroom. She had been the first pupil to come to me for coaching after school, and I'd become very fond of her

I lifted up one of her long blonde plaits to inspect beneath it.

"Your ears look fine to me. Why, have you got earache?"

Jemima took her plait from my hand and replaced it carefully over her shoulder.

"No, silly, not my real ears. My bunny ears. I had blue flowery ones, and I lost them somewhere on Friday. I thought I'd left them at school, but they weren't there today, nor in the playpark. So I thought I might have left them here after school when we came in to get milkshakes."

Blue flowery bunny ears. I bit my lip.

"You mean the sort of ears Carol makes to sell in the village shop for Easter?"

"Yes, that's right. Easter Bunny ears. I particularly chose those ones because my favourite colour is sapphire."

Her lessons were doing wonders for her vocabulary as well as her reading confidence.

"Small flowers or big ones?" I was hoping against hope that hers weren't the ones we'd found on Bunny.

"Miniscule ones."

I hesitated. That wasn't the answer I wanted to hear.

"Perhaps the easiest thing would be to ask Carol to make you another pair exactly the same as the ones you lost. She might still have some of the same material in her ragbag." Carol made the ears of out of scraps, ensuring an excellent profit margin as well an appealing variety. "In the meantime, I'll keep an eye out for them, and if I find them, I'll keep them for you until our next lesson. Now, what page did you get up to last week?"

I looked pointedly at my watch, hoping she wouldn't notice its battery had run out, to hint that we should focus on what her mother was paying me for. Our half hour lesson always flew by, even when we weren't diverted.

Jemima flipped open *Matilda* at her bookmark and began to read, but I didn't hear the first few paragraphs, too distracted by the fate of her ears. I hoped the village grapevine would never reveal the truth to this innocent little girl. Thank goodness Bunny had survived. It would have been so much worse for Jemima if Bunny's fall had been fatal.

As usual, Hector called through to me when our half-hour was up. Jemima and I returned to the public part of the shop to find her mother contentedly reading a novel in the tearoom. A new book, tea and cake were a voluntary tax frequently paid by my pupils' parents while they waited for their child's reading lesson to finish. No wonder Hector was happy to let me use the stockroom for free.

Jemima ran across to her mother, handed over her book bag, and went to the counter to collect a free lollipop from Hector, a lure he insisted on giving my pupils as a reward after each lesson. I worried that reading would prove bad for their teeth.

As her mother got out her purse to pay me for the lesson, I said, loudly enough for Jemima to hear, "I was just saying to your daughter, we haven't found her bunny ears in the shop, but we'll let you know if we come across them." With my back to Jemima, I widened my eyes as a warning, to see whether her mother knew the truth about where they'd been found. Her mother grimaced and gave a scarcely perceptible shake of the head. So she knew too.

"Jemima, let's pop into the shop on our way home, and we'll ask Carol to make you some more exactly the same," she said to her daughter.

"That's just what Sophie suggested," said Jemima, with a knowing look to Hector, seeking empathy at the frustrating conspiracies between grown-up ladies. But they left happily enough, Jemima holding her mother's hand and engaging her in deep conversation as they went up the High Street. I was left wondering what had become of Jemima's ears when Bunny was taken off in the ambulance. I took comfort from the thought that they'd have brightened up the day for the patients and staff in the accident and emergency department. Perhaps they were still at the hospital in Bunny's bedside locker. I wondered whether we should hand them in to the police, along with the fur coat and pink slippers. A bit of hard evidence might prompt them to take the incident seriously at last. On the other hand, that might do more

115

harm than good. After all, what could they prove? That Jemima was somehow involved in Bunny's bizarre disguise? She was hardly the Artful Dodger. And I still had no idea who the fur coat belonged to.

"Sophie, could you log these arrivals into stock while I cash up, please?"

I took the laptop, scanner and the small box of books over to a tearoom table and worked my way through them. They were all specials that we'd ordered at customers' specific requests. I remembered a pleasant teenager ordering the study guide for *Macbeth*, which was on the GCSE English syllabus that year. One of the primary school mums had asked for the fancy gift edition of *The Wind in the Willows*. But I drew a blank at the next book: *How to Plan a Funeral*. It was the only order of the three that I hadn't taken myself.

"Who's this for, Hector?" I held it up to show him.

Hector stopped counting pound coins. "I don't know. Not one of mine. Becky must have taken that order on Friday."

"Becky?" I didn't know Becky had been helping in the shop. She'd only helped out once before, in a crisis. "What was Becky doing here on Friday?"

Hector looked away. "Don't you remember? You had the morning off to go to the dentist. I got her in to cover for you, so I didn't lose writing time."

During quiet moments, Hector would work on his latest novel behind the trade counter. Would he have told me about Becky coming in if I hadn't asked about the funeral book? Was he planning for Becky to become a regular part of our team?

Hector hauled the order book down from the shelf behind him and flicked it open at the previous week's page. He ran his finger down the list.

"Yep, it's one of Becky's."

One of Becky's? So she was a master saleswoman now too, was she?

"So who's it for?" My pen was poised over the reservation ticket to slip inside the cover.

Hector's eyes widened as his finger stopped at the right order line.

"Miss Carter. It was ordered on Friday, by Kitty, presumably. Over the phone."

Thoughts of Becky vanished like a flame beneath a candle-snuffer.

"Goodness, do you think that means she was planning to kill Bunny all along?"

Hector slipped the last of the coins into a plastic bag.

"If she was, she'd be daft to incriminate herself like that. Besides, considering she's Bunny's carer, and Bunny is getting on a bit, it's not unreasonable to order a book like that. Personally, I'd be more suspicious if a person with no ageing relatives asked for it."

"Maybe it was ordered by someone pretending to be Kitty, to place the blame on her? The real perpetrator trying to cover his or her own tracks?"

Hector shrugged. "There aren't many customers who order books from us by phone. They usually either come into the shop or bypass us and order books from online retailers in the comfort of their own home. Kitty and Bunny have never got their heads round the internet, nor do they leave the house. Which is why they're an exception."

"If someone wanted to set Kitty up, it would be easy to fake a phone order. It might even have been Bunny.

Their voices are very similar. If Becky had never met either of them, she would take on trust whatever name the person on the other end of the phone gave her."

"Next thing, you'll be telling me that Paul or Stuart did it, faking a high voice to pretend to be Kitty. But why would they do that?"

"There's one way to find out. We'll ask Kitty, and if she claims she has no knowledge of it, we'll know it was a hoax."

Hector piled the moneybags into the safe and set the combination while I powered down the laptop.

"Or else it's a double bluff. She could deny all knowledge so as to suggest someone else is trying to frame her. But is Kitty smart enough to think that up? I wonder."

20 All Change

A lean businessman I didn't know, still handsome though his face was lined beyond his middle-aged years, brandished a fifty-pound note at me across the trade counter.

"Could you kindly change this into one-pound coins?"

His lips were so tightly pursed, I could hardly see them.

"I'm sorry, I don't have that many pound coins in the till," I replied. "My boss has just cashed up and gone to the bank. I'm only still here because I'm setting up for the Writers' Group meeting this evening."

If he'd bought a book or even a greetings card and asked for pound coins in the change, I'd have been more cooperative.

"Well, I need some pound coins now for a parking meter." He pointed out of the window to a shiny black Lexus parked outside the shop.

"Fifty of them? That's expensive parking! Where's that? Not here, obviously. We don't have any parking meters in Wendlebury Barrow. We don't even have yellow lines."

I sat down on Hector's stool and folded my arms. The man's eyes darted this way and that, looking everywhere but at me.

"They're for later, in town," he said quickly. "A few of them, anyway. What I mostly need them for is—" his face brightened. "—is a penny mile the vicar's doing as a fundraiser. You know, where you ask people to lay down coins in a long line as a way of donating them to your charity."

That was news to me. I pulled the shop's copy of the parish magazine out from under the counter and turned to the church news page. No sign of any fundraisers there. I looked the stranger in the eye.

"That's funny, I'd have thought the vicar would have mentioned his penny mile to me. I teach Sunday School for him, you know." I might not have started there yet, but I wanted to assert my authority. "However, I'll be seeing him on Sunday, so if you'd like to leave your donation with me, I'll be sure to give it to him then. I can change it into coins from the till at the end of trading on Saturday."

I smiled sweetly and reached for his banknote. He snatched it away and stuffed it back into his pocket.

"No, no, don't worry. I'll catch him later. I'll come back." Remembering his manners, and perhaps a little embarrassed at being caught out in an obvious lie, he backed away towards the travel section. "Perhaps I'll just have a browse while I'm here."

I took the opportunity to examine his features in profile – the lean, slightly horsey face and the aquiline nose. Surely this was one of Bunny's children? There was a touch of Paul's snideness about him as well, though he lacked his brother's arrogance.

"I thought for a moment you had come to collect a book order." I indicated the specials shelf behind me, where all the fulfilled orders stood, awaiting collection. I pulled out the funeral book at random and held it up to show him.

"Funeral planning? What would I want with a book about funeral planning? I'm sorry, you must be mixing me up with someone else."

He looked genuinely baffled.

The cadence of his voice matched Paul's, as did his accent, in common with half the village. Could this be Stuart? His hands had the same long, tapering fingers that Bunny had wrapped around the volume of John Clare's poems, though his were as yet unbent by arthritis.

"If you don't mind me asking, are you Mrs Carter's son?"

His face clouded. "Yes, I'm Stuart Brady, her youngest son. How did you know? And why do you ask?"

When I glanced involuntarily at the funeral book on the counter, he turned pale.

"You mean – you don't mean – she's not dead, is she?"

I had not intended to frighten him. I meant only to assess whether he might have faked Kitty's order for the funeral book.

"I'm sorry, I didn't mean to alarm you. She's as well as can be expected under the circumstances. At least she was when I went to visit her in hospital on Sunday morning."

He laid a hand on the counter to steady himself. "What's she doing in hospital?"

If he was feigning ignorance, he was doing an impressive job of it. Why had Paul and Kitty not told their brother about their mother's accident?

"She had a fall." I was pleased with myself on improvising such a diplomatic yet truthful answer. "She's in Ward 27 if you want to go and see her."

He replaced the book he was holding and thrust his hand back into his pocket for the fifty-pound note, his eyes brightening. "Oh, well then, I'll be needing some pound coins for the hospital car park." He held it out to me again, more expectantly than before.

Although I could have broken in to the next day's float, something told me not to comply. Had I subconsciously noticed the note was a fake? We didn't take many fifties in the shop, and I seldom had any in my purse, so I wasn't familiar with them. Then I realised I could easily bypass the problem.

"Don't worry, you won't need coins to park at the hospital. It's all done by card with a number-plate recognition system. You don't even need a paper ticket. Just flash your credit or debit card as you leave."

His shoulders sagged as he stashed the note away again. It looked as if it was the only banknote he had. Perhaps he wasn't as flush as I'd first thought.

"Were you planning to visit your mother at home tonight? Is that why you are in Wendlebury? I'm sorry if you've had a wasted journey."

"I was coming to meet my brother, Paul." His left eye twitched.

"At your mother's house?"

"At The Bluebird. He told me he wanted to meet on neutral territory to discuss my mother. I suppose he means without my mother or half-sister present."

"Wouldn't it have been easier to meet in Slate Green?"

His eye twitched again, and he put up his hand to still it.

"I suppose so, but I've been away from the place more often than not lately. On business, you know. Still, Paul asked me to come to Wendlebury, so here I am. Though it will feel odd to be back in The Bluebird." He gave a wan smile. "Old haunts from my youth. I can't remember the last time I had a drink there. I don't suppose Paul does, either."

"He's been at The Bluebird a lot over the last few days." I watched Stuart closely to assess his reaction. "The landlord's hired him to do some building work on his new courtyard garden. I expect he's been working there today."

"Unlike him to get his hands dirty. That'll do him good. I wondered why he was asking me to meet him so early. I thought the pub wouldn't open till six. I suppose Paul will be knocking off for the day about now."

I glanced at the clock on the wall, conscious that I still hadn't set up the Writers' Group meeting, and he took the hint.

"Well, I'd better be getting along, then. Thanks for your help. Sorry, I didn't catch your name."

"I'm Sophie Sayers," I said. I was glad we were parting on friendly terms, even though I hadn't given in about the pound coins.

"Thanks, Sophie."

When he plunged a hand into his trouser pockets to retrieve his car keys, a multitude of coins jangled, as if he'd just hit the jackpot on a fruit machine. How much parking was the man planning to do that night?

As soon as he'd left, I closed the door and locked it behind him.

21 Overheard

Just as the Writers' Group was wrapping up its discussion about our spring readings event, an altercation in the street interrupted the conversation. It was getting louder, heading up the High Street towards Hector's House from the direction of The Bluebird.

"You're an embarrassment, Stuart," snapped a familiar voice. "If you must play those wretched machines, play them well away from here."

The gruff response was unintelligible.

"Just when I've been getting on so well with the landlord too. And think of poor Mother. How is she going to feel when she knows her son's been banned from her local for breaking a fruit machine?" So that's what he wanted the pound coins for. "You always were a bad loser. You were just the same when we were kids, playing Monopoly. You could never bear it when I won. You even taught Kitty to play before she was old enough to think strategically, just so you could beat her."

They came to a halt beside Stuart's car. As the lights were out at the front of the shop, they must have presumed there was no-one in it.

"Sounds like the Brady brothers," said Dinah.

Karen started taking notes. "That's given me a great idea for a short story: how childhood games morph into adult problems. Do you think that's why Stuart Brady became an accountant and Paul a builder? Childhood battles over the Monopoly board?"

"Shhh!"

We all craned towards the window to hear better.

"Don't kid yourself you're suddenly the expert on family relationships," Stuart was saying. "When you phoned to arrange to meet tonight, you didn't even think to tell me Mum was ill."

"If you visited her more often, you'd have found out for yourself. You only ever go to see her when you're broke. It's pathetic, a grown man still sponging off his mother. What would Father say if he were still alive? What would your clients say if they knew?"

"You're in no position to take the moral high ground. You're only here to lobby people about your get-rich-quick schemes, not for Mum's benefit at all. Mum would have forty fits if she knew what you were up to."

Paul's tone changed to defensive. "It's only because I've got her best interests at heart."

"Best interests, my arse," said Stuart. "You're just after a fast buck."

There was an icy silence, inside the shop and out.

"What do you know about business interests?" retorted Paul. "You and your supposed business trips! What accountant does that much work away from his office? Playing away, more like. No wonder you're always skint. As if throwing cash at fruit machines wasn't wasteful enough."

I thought Stuart might thump him. Instead he opened his car door and slid into the driver's seat. I hoped neither of them had been drinking alcohol.

"If you expect me to support your scheme for the Manor House, you can think again," said Stuart. "You're on your own."

Stuart slammed the car door, started the engine, and, with a crunching of gears, pulled away, leaving Paul standing alone on the pavement, his hands folded tightly across his chest.

Through the half light of the shop, we watched Paul's face illuminated briefly by the flame of a cigarette lighter as he ignited a long, slim cigar. He inhaled and exhaled a couple of lungfuls of smoke, before turning back in the direction of the pub, where presumably he'd left his car.

The silence was broken by Jessica.

"Well, that explains it. I wondered why Stuart kept coming back to the Cats Prevention tombola at the Village Show last summer. I spent an hour helping on their stall in the afternoon, and he couldn't stay away. I was starting to think he might fancy me, as he was buying so many tickets. He won some nice prizes, but gave most of them back, saying he had no use for them. Perhaps he wanted to hide the evidence of how many tickets he'd bought. Or maybe he just liked the thrill of the chase."

"I trust Donald will get rid of the fruit machine now," said Dinah. "I've been on at him for ages about being a gambling enabler, but he won't listen. Says he needs the profit. If he wants to attract families to his new beer garden, he needs to change his tune."

"Sounds as if he'll have to get rid of this machine anyway. Perhaps Stuart's done us all a favour by breaking it."

"Honestly, you'd think being an accountant he'd be more savvy," said Dinah. "With slot machines, the odds are always stacked against the players."

"We all believe what we want to be true," said Jessica. "I know I do."

"Well, I feel sorry for him," said Bella. "It's not entirely his fault. Addictive personalities run through his family. His father used to spend a fortune betting on dominoes, and there's Kitty's old problem with drink and drugs, though I've heard that's under control since she's been back living with her mother."

"And what's Bunny's addiction?" I asked.

"Having children," said Dinah. "Ten of them. Can you imagine? I reckon that's why she was so keen on having that reprobate Kitty back to live with her. Kitty still needs mothering."

"I thought Kitty was Bunny's carer?" I asked.

"So Kitty would like to believe. But I reckon it's as much the other way round."

"Sometimes I'm glad I'm an only child," I said. "Although I always wanted to be a twin when I was little, or at least have a sister near my own age who was just like me."

"How funny if you were a twin, then your twin could marry Hector's twin brother, Horace," said Jessica, clapping her hands with glee. "I wonder whether Mr Murray's ever officiated at a double wedding before?"

I started to clear away the cups. It was time to draw the meeting to a swift close.

22 Escape at Elevenses

When Billy entered Hector's House at the crack of elevenses, he kept his right hand stuffed in his trouser pocket, trying to still something that was moving about. I could see the outline of his knuckles through the sagging tweed, but not what he was holding. Had we been in a city centre, I might have feared he was about to pull out a gun and raid the till, but when he approached the trade counter, he produced nothing more threatening than a kitten.

The tiny thing was still young enough for its short, soft black fur to defy gravity. Sticking straight up from the kitten's fragile body, it gave the little creature an air of permanent surprise. Or maybe that was just the effect of being transported in Billy's trousers.

Hector took a step back from the counter. "I'm sorry, Billy, we only accept pounds sterling. But if you try the village shop, Carol will probably give you a good exchange rate on kittens."

I set down the teacup I was drying and dashed over to join them. Picking up the tiny creature with both hands and holding her close to my chest, I could feel her miniature heart pounding against mine. I ran a soothing finger down her spine, her coat as soft as a dandelion clock about to blow.

"Oh, Billy, she's gorgeous! What's her name?"

Wiping his hands on his trousers, Billy shuffled over to his usual tearoom table.

"I don't know, it hasn't said."

I followed him, still holding the kitten.

"But she is yours, isn't she? Or did you find her as a stray?"

He shrugged. "It ain't anybody's. Catwoman brought it round. It just appeared on Kitty's kitchen table first thing this morning. When Catwoman stepped out to use the lavvy, Kitty threw a saucepan at it, so I thought I'd better take it out of harm's way."

The kitten wriggled out of my grasp and climbed up to my shoulder, digging in claws as sharp as needles, before nestling down amongst my hair. Snuggling into the crook of my neck beneath my left ear, she began purring louder than I'd have thought possible for her size.

"Look, she likes me!" I sat down slowly in the chair opposite Billy, not wanting to disturb her. "Where did she come from?"

"Another cat, I'm guessing."

Hector kept his distance behind the trade counter. "We can't have a cat in the tearoom, Sophie. It's unhygienic."

Billy eyed the cake stands. "And it's stopping Sophie from making my tea. I'll have my usual, please, girlie."

I put a protective hand to my shoulder to stop the kitten falling. Her purring stopped, only to be replaced by the cutest snore I'd ever heard.

"Hector, please fetch me the smallest cardboard box you can find in the stockroom, and some of that

130

crumpled paper packaging from the recycling box. Little Pussykins here needs a nest for her morning nap."

Holding her firmly on my shoulder, I got up to switch on the kettle, while Hector, muttering to himself, found a box and lined it with packaging. I lowered her in gently without disturbing her slumber.

"There, that'll make her return journey more comfortable, Billy. You can just close the box lid till you get home."

Billy sat back abruptly and raised his hands in protest. "I'm not taking it home with me. Nor back to Kitty's neither. It needs a safer place than that, poor little mite."

"I thought Bunny liked taking in cats?" said Hector.

I filled a teapot for Billy. "Besides, you'd think a kitten would trump cats. What's not to love about a kitten?"

"Kitty don't like 'em," said Billy. "She gives short shrift to that wretched Catwoman when Bunny's not listening. If it was down to Catwoman, the Manor House would be full of moggies. Left to Kitty, they'd all be six feet under. The cats, I mean, not the women. Though maybe Catwoman too."

I'd clocked that Kitty wasn't exactly fond of her feline residents, but I hadn't marked her down for catricide.

"Catwoman's with her right now, trying to win round Kitty in Bunny's absence. That's why I came out for a breath of fresh air. I left them to slug it out between them. I couldn't take all the bloody swearing."

"So did the kitten follow you of her own accord, or did you catnap her?" I reached a finger into the box to touch her little furry head.

"No, I just scooped it up and slipped it in my pocket before Kitty could do it any more harm."

I set the full teapot down on the table and lingered to stroke the kitten again before fetching Billy's toast.

"Isn't that woman's charity meant to be about neutering cats?" said Hector. "She can't be much good at it, if she has to keep rehoming unwanted kittens."

"Unwanted kitten?" I grinned. "Isn't that a contradiction in terms? How could anyone see this little soul and not want to give her a good home?"

Hector looked so horrified that you'd think I'd suggested serving her to Billy on his toast.

"Well, I wouldn't for a start," said Hector. "You can't have a pet in a flat. It isn't fair on the animal. Besides, it would make a mess of my stuff."

"And I'm not taking up cat keeping at my time of life," said Billy, reaching out to stroke the kitten's ears.

I wasn't convinced. On Sunday afternoon, he'd looked right at home sleeping with Kitty's cats on his lap.

"There's a good chance it would see me out," he went on, as if trying to convince himself. "Besides, if I was going to get a cat, I should get a dog instead. Something sensible that could go out and about with me."

"I'd get a breed that likes digging, if I were you, Billy," said Hector. "Something substantial like a Golden Retriever or a Labrador. Or how about a terrier? They go at holes like – well, like terriers. I can picture you with a nice Jack Russell. It would make light work of gravedigging for you. I've always fancied having a Border Collie myself."

I'd never put Hector down as a dog man before.

"Yes, and it would wreck my garden too," said Billy. I suspected he was more of a ferret man.

I laid protective hands over the kitten's ears. "Don't listen to these nasty men, Fluffy."

Billy poured some tea into his cup as I went to fetch a jug of milk and some of Hector's special alcoholic cream. Billy hesitated before choosing the milk. Perhaps a few days with the addle-brained Kitty was making him reflect on his own unhealthy lifestyle. But all he did with it was pour a little into his saucer and set it beside the box for the kitten, before topping up his tea with cream.

"Bunny would keep it, if she was at home," he said, lifting the kitten out of her box for a drink. "But Kitty's bent on getting rid of as many cats as she can before her mother comes back. She's like Pol Pot in there."

"Not famed for his love of cats," said Hector. "Won't Bunny be upset when she comes home and finds out?"

"Most likely she won't even notice, there's so many of them lurking about the house. I swear Catwoman brings a new one every time she visits."

"It must be costing Bunny a fortune in cat food, quite apart from whatever donations Mrs Lot squeezes out of her." Hector was ever practical.

I slid a finger underneath the kitten's abdomen. "Not for this one. Look, her tummy's no bigger than a matchbox."

"No worries on that score," said Billy. "They're self-sufficient with all those mice in the Manor House, not to mention the rats and birds in the garden. And if I finds any dead mice in my cottage, I always save them and take them round to help out. I don't like to see animals suffer, not even moggies."

"Well, I'll be happy to take this little one off their hands." With droplets of milk clinging to her whiskers, the kitten jumped back into her box. I picked it up and took it over to the tearoom counter to keep an eye on her.

"You can't keep it there, Sophie," said Hector. "This is a shop, not a ship."

"It would keep your mice under control," said Billy, coming round to my side.

Hector frowned. "Yes, just like my elephant gun keeps away stray elephants. We don't have any mice in this shop, thank you very much."

"Nor do I in my house," I said. "But that's not the reason I'm offering to adopt her. I just fancy having a cat. A constant and loyal companion, something warm and welcoming to come home to."

Billy shot a mischievous look at Hector and opened his mouth to speak, but Hector got in first.

"OK, take it home at lunchtime. Otherwise when the kids come in after school they'll terrorise it with their affections."

I stroked the little creature, proud to be her new owner.

"What shall I call her?"

"How about Kitty?" said Billy.

I laughed. "That might cause confusion."

"How about Satan?" said Hector.

I carried her around the shop in her box, looking at the bookshelves for inspiration, thinking to name her after an author or a book. I hoped she might miaow when we passed something suitable.

Then the door creaked open, and a customer came in, followed by a few delicate petals of pale pink blossom blowing in from next door's garden.

"Blossom," I said straight away. "I think I'll call her Blossom. She's about as light as a flower petal anyway, and I think Auntie May would approve. It suits her already. Perfect."

Hector turned his attention to the customer.

"I can drop it in at yours after I leave here, if you like," said Billy. "I'm going back up the Manor House once Catwoman's gone. A kitten won't last long in there up

134

against Kitty. If I take it out of the box, it'll just fit nicely through your letterbox."

"Billy, you'll do no such thing! I'll take Blossom home myself at lunchtime, as Hector says. But if you want to be helpful, you can deliver a book to Kitty that's just come in for her. Apparently she ordered it over the phone last Friday."

"I'm surprised she used the phone," said Billy. "She don't much like making or taking phone calls."

"Yes, Bunny usually phones herself if she wants anything," said Hector.

Billy looked glum. "Kitty don't even like her voice leaving the house these days, never mind her body. It beats me how she hasn't got rickets, with barely a drop of sunshine on her body from one day to the next."

I looked at Hector, hesitating, until he gave me a slight nod of agreement to spill the beans.

"Are you sure about that, Billy? We think she does go outdoors. In fact, we know she does, because when we called round on Sunday and found you asleep, she was out in the garden gathering herbs to make mint sauce."

Billy spluttered into his tea cup. "Herbs? Is that what she told you? I wouldn't fancy her kind of herbs poured over my Sunday dinner. Though I suppose they might make me enjoy her terrible cooking a bit more."

Hector grinned. "Oh, that kind of herbs! Does she claim they're medicinal?"

Billy chuckled. "They're about as likely to come on prescription as this here cream." He held up the jug of Hector's hooch, before succumbing to temptation and tipping a small amount into his second cup of tea.

Hector laughed. "No wonder she covered up the basket so fast when she saw us. The shape of the leaves would have given her game away."

"Which herbs are they?" I asked. "I like rosemary." With its sharp, astringent fragrance, this spiny-needled herb had long been my favourite in Auntie May's herb garden.

"Pot plants," said Hector.

"What, you mean like aspidistra?" I named the plant at random, having shelved a copy of George Orwell's *Keep the Aspidistra Flying* that morning. I'd always wondered what an aspidistra looked like and was glad to have seen one on the book's cover. My job is so educational.

Hector lowered his voice, even though we were the only ones in the shop. "No, you twit, marijuana."

"Oh. Oh, I see."

For a moment I felt sorry for Kitty. All that time and trouble that Billy had spent on the vast walled garden at the Manor House, the kind of garden my Auntie May would have killed for, and the only pleasure Kitty could extract from it came from what she could smoke out of it.

Billy got up to pet the kitten one last time before he left. "Don't feel so bad, girlie. It took me a while to catch on to why she didn't want me to do any weeding in her special little glasshouse out the back. She told me at first she was raising an exotic variant of camomile, grown from seeds given to her by a Turkish tightrope walker. A proper camomile lawn is a wonderful thing, smells beautiful, it does, with every step you take, so I encouraged her." He reached into the box and gently lifted Blossom's tail. "Once the leaves of Kitty's seedlings started to differentiate, I knew they weren't no camomile leaves. But it wasn't doing me no harm, and it was the only thing that ever got her to leave the house, so I left her to it."

He shuffled over to collect the book from Hector. As he reached the counter, he turned to call over his shoulder to me.

"By the way, girlie, you might want to know little Blossom there is actually a boy."

My mouth fell open in surprise.

"So, the book order, then." Hector hauled the conversation back on track, holding up the cover for Billy to read. Billy squinted, struggling to make out the title at that distance without his reading glasses. As Hector read it out to him, Billy's eyes widened in surprise.

"*How to Plan a Funeral?* When did you say she ordered it again?"

"On Friday morning," said Hector. "The day before her mother was left for dead in your grave."

23 Asleep at the Wheel

After Billy had gone, I finished calling the other customers whose orders had just come in, then the phone rang. The speed-dial directory told me the call was from Bunny Carter's landline. As I braced myself for a telephone conversation with Kitty, it occurred to me that if she hadn't ordered the funeral planning book, Billy's delivering it to her could look like a tasteless practical joke.

"It's Catwoman," said a gruff male voice that I recognised at once.

"You can't fool me, I know that's Billy. What on earth are you playing at?"

"I mean Catwoman is in trouble."

"What do you want me to do, call Batman?" I put my hand over the mouthpiece and called out to Hector, who was packing up returns in the stock room. "Hector! Time to get out your Batmobile!"

Billy tutted. "Listen, girlie, don't mess me about. This is serious. That pesky Catwoman is sitting outside Kitty's house, slumped over the steering wheel of her car, snoring her head off."

"That sounds a bit odd. Is she OK?"

"Why do you think I'm calling you, you daftie? The car door wasn't locked, so I opened it and prodded her with a stick, but she didn't respond. Then I sounded her horn, and she didn't flinch. I think she's more than just asleep."

"If she's snoring, she must be breathing."

"Loud as a donkey's bray, and about as musical."

Hector emerged from the stockroom. "Did you call, Girl Wonder? What's up, is an urgent delivery needed? Someone who can't wait another moment to read the book they've ordered?"

I held up my hand to shush him while Billy continued.

"I'd call 999, but she don't look ill. More like drunk, though she don't smell of drink. Besides, I don't want to get her arrested."

I felt no sympathy for her.

"If she was planning to drive in that state, she deserves to get arrested."

Hector came to stand close behind me.

"Not Kitty?" he whispered, and I shook my head.

"Wait there, Billy. I'll send Hector. Go and stand by her car to keep an eye on her, and he'll be with you in a minute. Bye."

I clicked 'end' and chucked Hector his car keys from the hook on the wall.

"So it's my turn for a mercy mission now."

I handed him his mobile phone. "You're always telling me a good bookshop should be a lynchpin of its local community. Now's your chance. Go commune. Billy has just found Mrs Lot insensible at the wheel of her car outside the Manor House. He thinks she's drunk, and he needs assistance to prise her out of there and sober her up."

Hector glanced at his diary, which lay open beside his laptop. "Rescuing drunks wasn't on my to-do list today, but as it's Billy asking, I'd better go." He hesitated. "You hold the fort, Sophie."

"Well, yes, obviously," I said to his departing back. Surely he wasn't thinking of calling Becky in to cover for his absence?

I was glad to be distracted by the arrival of a tourist wanting advice on books about the Cotswolds. She must have wondered why I pulled out a book on Cumbria by mistake and dropped three maps on the floor in succession. Just as she left with a book of local walks under her arm, Hector returned, parking his Land Rover on the street instead of in its usual place at the side of the shop. He came back into shop and gave me a hasty progress report.

"Don't worry, she's OK, but she's definitely not fit to drive. Dr Perkins is taking her home."

"Dr Perkins? So Billy didn't call 999?"

"No, by coincidence, Dr Perkins was just walking past the Manor House as I arrived. Apparently he used to be Mrs Lot's GP. He said he thought she had accidentally overdosed on cough mixture. He found an empty bottle of codeine linctus in her bag." Hector brandished a large calico tote bag advertising the Cats Prevention charity. "Dr Perkins said it's a common addiction, because it's easy to buy the stuff over the counter in this country. In America and other places, it's banned, because it contains an opiate."

I grinned. "I can imagine getting addicted to cough mixture. It always tastes so delicious, not like a medicine at all."

"That's half the trouble, apparently. People don't realise they're hooked till it's too late."

"So what are you doing with her bag?"

"Dr Perkins left it on the pavement by mistake. Between him, Billy and me, we managed to move her across to the passenger seat, so Dr Perkins could drive her home in her own car. He'll stay with her till she wakes up to make sure she's OK and to give her advice on how to break the habit."

"That's kind of him, considering he's meant to be retired."

"Once you've spent your whole career caring for people, it must be hard to turn off that habit like a tap. When I retire from the shop, I'm sure I'll still be recommending books to people to read."

He'd never spoken about his long-term future before. The idea of thirty years ahead of him selling books in Hector's House didn't seem to daunt him at all. I felt the shop walls start to close in on me.

"So how will he get back?"

"He's going to text me when he's ready, and I'll collect him in the Land Rover and bring him home."

Whistling along to *Carnival of the Animals*, which he'd set playing when Billy produced the kitten, Hector returned to the stockroom to pick up where he'd left off, leaving Mrs Lot's bag on the counter, along with his car keys. I hung up his keys on the hook where he liked to keep them, then, as I turned round, I sent the bag flying with my elbow.

I seemed to be having a clumsy day. I exclaimed aloud, then knelt to pick up the contents, glad there were no full bottles of cough medicine left in the bag, or there'd have been a sticky mess.

Having gathered up the inevitable Cats Prevention flyers and will leaflets, a few paw print badges, and a notebook and pen, I stood up and nearly slipped over, skidding on a small plastic zip-lock bag containing some dried green leaves. Catnip, perhaps?

I'd never seen catnip in action but had heard the effects were comical. Would Blossom be old enough to try it? Or was there a feline equivalent for catnip to the legal age limit for tobacco or alcohol? I wondered whether it might have any effect on people.

Hector reappeared in search of parcel tape just as I was tipping some of the catnip out into my hand.

"Sophie, what on earth are you thinking?" He stayed my hand as I was just about to raise the catnip to my nose to sniff it.

"It's catnip. I just found it in Mrs Lot's bag."

Hector gave a hollow laugh. "You're not a habitual user of catnip, then?"

"No. Why?"

"Oh, Sophie, don't you know what that is? Look at the shape of the leaves. Doesn't that remind you of anything?"

I considered the leaves, flattening the biggest one in the palm of my hand. This plant wasn't in my aunt's garden.

"Conker trees? The Canadian flag? Maple syrup?"

"Did your travels with Damian never take you to the cafés of Amsterdam?"

He reached behind me to the sound system, and within a few seconds, Bob Marley and the Wailers were making the shelves vibrate.

"Ah!" I said, my eyes widening.

He reduced the volume to background level. "And for my next question: what was marijuana doing in Mrs Lot's bag?"

"Medical use? At her age, surely it must be for medical purposes?"

143

Hector smiled. "Very generous of you, Sophie, though ageist. But more importantly, does this mean Kitty is her dealer?"

24 A Brother Scorned

Only when I was on my way home after work did I realise that in all the drama over Mrs Lot's collapse, we still hadn't pinned down whether Kitty really had ordered the funeral book. I needed a pretext for calling in to see Kitty to find out whether it had been her.

Paul provided the solution. As I passed my front gate, steeling myself to turn up the path to the Manor House, he came charging out of the front door, slamming it behind him and crossing the porch in a single stride. He scowled as he saw me approach.

"What are you doing here, busybody?"

Gone was the wheedling tone he'd used when he thought I might sell him my cottage.

I smiled sweetly. "Just being neighbourly. I wanted to check Kitty was all right, as there was an unfortunate incident with her visitor earlier today. I was worried in case she was upset.

"Upset? I should say so. When is she not upset about something? I heard all about that cat woman being rescued by the doctor. God knows what Kitty did to her."

He went to push past me, but I planted my feet apart, hands on hips, to block his way. He'd have had to physically assault me to get to the front gate.

"Kitty didn't do anything to her. It was self-inflicted."

"What do you know about medical matters? You're only a waitress."

I felt my heartbeat speed up.

"I'm a trained teacher and just as much a professional as Dr Perkins. Which is more than can be said of a mere builder who wasn't there."

I hadn't intended to say 'mere' but it just slipped out.

"You cheeky cow. I make a damn sight more money than you do. And I have my own successful business, rather than riding on someone else's coat-tails. You're as much of a parasite as my layabout half-sister in there, who hasn't done a day's work for years. She can't even be bothered to go as far as the village shop. Talk about lazy!"

Although Paul had slammed the front door, I noticed it had rebounded and stood ajar. I was surprised he hadn't noticed it was broken and fixed it, being a builder. Then the door moved slightly. Kitty must have been behind it, listening. I raised my voice, just in case.

"She can't help her agoraphobia. That's a medical condition. Criticising it would be like saying Dr Perkins is lazy because he wears glasses rather than being bothered to use his eyes properly."

"Agoraphobia, my eye. More that my mother won't let her out on her own for fear of the trouble she'd get into."

"It still means she's not fit to care for herself, never mind my mother." The door moved to narrow the gap. "The sooner I get this place converted into a proper care home, the better."

146

I could not believe his lack of respect for the feelings for his half-sister, but in his next breath, he revealed a grain of compassion for her.

"She'd be better off out from under my mother's feet, anyway. Mother is just her enabler, treating her like a child. I hate to think how much of Mother's money she drinks away."

"Kitty doesn't drink at all these days. Not alcohol, anyway. I've never seen her drunk in my life."

I crossed my fingers that he wasn't going to ask me how many times I had met her. I hoped he'd assume we'd been friends ever since I moved to Wendlebury. Truth be told, I was feeling guilty that I hadn't hooked up with her before now. Strange that my aunt had never introduced us. Perhaps she feared Kitty might lead me astray. I would probably have felt the same in her place.

At that point Billy strolled around the side of the house from the back garden, pushing a rusty wheelbarrow. At the sight of Paul, he went straight back to wherever he'd come from. But he wasn't quick enough to escape unseen.

"What with that old layabout sponging off my mother as well, it's little wonder she has no spare money to keep the estate in order. Kitty's father left her the house, you know, but no money for its maintenance. It's falling in value by the minute, thanks to their neglect."

I wondered whether his childhood home had been humbler and his father less affluent than Kitty's.

"At least Billy keeps the garden in order." To be fair, it was very neat and tidy. "And the vicar told me Billy's charges are fair and reasonable. He gardens for the vicar too."

But Paul didn't want to talk about Billy.

"I suppose you've got a vested interest in visiting my mother too. What is it, building up business for your precious bookshop? As if she hasn't already got too many books in the house. You're as bad as that charity woman, cornering her in her own home, demanding cash donations and dumping stray cats on her. Clear off, and don't come scrounging off my mother and sister again."

So much for the half-sister. She was full family when it suited him.

"How dare you?" I didn't mean to defend Mrs Lot, but I was too riled to disentangle the strands of his abuse. "Perhaps while you're living the high life down in Slate Green, you've forgotten what it's like to be neighbourly, to care about those around you for their own sake, without any thought of personal gain?"

Paul's eyes narrowed as he folded his arms across his chest.

"I think you're forgetting I was born and raised in Wendlebury Barrow. I am far more the villager than you will ever be. You've only lived here five minutes, so don't go lecturing me about village life."

"Being neighbourly isn't a question of how long you've lived somewhere. It's a matter of human kindness. You don't need to have Wendlebury Barrow on your birth certificate to pick up its spirit."

"Or to pick up its eligible bachelors. I notice it hasn't taken you five minutes to get stuck into that ponce Munro." He leaned closer to me, too close for comfort, with a suggestive leer. "Or for him to get stuck into you."

I shrank back in disgust, which gave him the chance to push past me and dash for the gate, before striding up the High Street in the direction of The Bluebird.

25 Good Neighbours

By now I was in no state to visit Kitty. Rather than provide comfort, I'd be more likely to alarm her. Besides, Billy was there. She didn't need me. The question of the funeral planning book could wait.

I turned to go home, bowing my head and letting my hair fall over my face to hide my angry tears. But I couldn't fool Joshua. As I reached my gate, he was picking ghostly pale narcissi in his front garden. I wondered how much he had heard.

"Good afternoon, my dear, you look as if you need a cup of tea. I was just about to have one myself. Do come and join me."

He opened his gate in welcome.

I usually try to avoid drinking his tea because his cups are never thoroughly washed, but his kindness was just what I needed. Besides, if he'd lived to be so old by drinking from dirty cups, they couldn't exactly be poisonous. As my Auntie May used to say, "We all have to eat a peck of dirt before we die". As a little girl, I'd assumed a peck was just enough dirt to fill a bird's beak. Now I know it means about nine litres, I don't worry so much.

Following Joshua through to his kitchen, the mirror image of mine, I chose a chair padded with a round orange cushion knitted with the pattern of a sunburst, a little touch of love left behind by his late wife. Auntie May was never a knitter.

He waited for me to begin the conversation as he busied himself filling the kettle and setting out cups and saucers. I knew he wouldn't pry, but would let me tell him as much or as little as I wished to disclose. Even just sitting with him in silence was comforting, knowing he was feeling my sadness and wanting to make it go away.

"It was that Paul Brady," I began. "I was just dropping by to check on Kitty when he made an unexpected attack on me. Not a physical attack—" Joshua looked relieved "—just horrible personal comments on my character and on my place in this village. He was nasty about Hector too." I spared Joshua the details. "He told me to go away and leave Kitty alone."

Joshua fumbled with the tea caddy, spilling tea leaves on the table as his hands shook from caddy to pot.

"A brother's natural protectiveness of his little sister?" Joshua's voice was gentle. I wondered whether he had ever had a younger sister. He would have made a great older brother.

I sniffed and blew my nose. "He was very rude about Kitty too. I've only met him twice, but each time he's been scathing about her ability to care for their mother."

Joshua took the teapot to the kettle.

"Kitty may not be the ideal carer for her mother, but at least she is there for her, all day, every day."

There was no trace of envy in his voice, but he must have wished he had a child to care for him in his old age. Would he rather have Kitty as a carer than his solitary life, pottering about his cottage alone as his faculties slowly failed?

Now I felt bad for criticising Kitty, and I sought to salve my conscience by speaking up for her.

"I gather she is the only one of Bunny's ten children to sacrifice her own independence for her mother's sake, and to give up her career."

Joshua's eyes twinkled as he replaced the lid on the teapot and slipped a knitted tea cosy into place. "I'd hardly call it a career, selling hotdogs from a van. But it was certainly the lifestyle she had chosen, touring music and farming festivals, and it was very sociable indeed. Dear May once drew on Kitty's comprehensive knowledge of festivals for a newspaper article she was writing. May liked her very much."

That did it for me. I would be firmly on Kitty's side now, whatever else might happen. Only one niggling worry remained.

"So you don't think it was Kitty who dumped her mother in that grave?"

Joshua chuckled. "Dear me, no. She should be the last person to fall under suspicion. If Kitty had designs on her mother's life, she could have taken a much simpler and less dramatic route at home. At Bunny's age, no-one would be surprised at a death from natural causes, simply not waking up in her bed one morning. And if she'd been under the doctor lately, there probably wouldn't even be a post-mortem."

He fetched the milk jug from the fridge.

"I thank my lucky stars that I inherited my parents' cottage, so I have no need to fear being forced out of the village. My declining years, when they come, will assuredly be spent here."

I was touched by the fact that he thought they hadn't started yet.

He settled himself on the chair opposite mine. "No, if there is one thing Kitty doesn't want, it's to lose her mother. Bunny's passing, when it comes, will be Kitty's worst nightmare. Unless Bunny's made a will to the contrary, the house will no doubt be sold for the proceeds to be shared between her surviving children. In consequence, Kitty will most likely have to leave the village. There are very few cottages small enough for one person in the village, and no council flats or cheap rentals for single people in Wendlebury, as you may have noticed. That's why there are virtually no eligible young men or women living in the village any longer."

As he concentrated on filling our cups from the teapot, I realised for the first time what a rarity I was in Wendlebury. But now, since Christmas, there was also Becky.

26 The Comfort of Cake

Fortified by Joshua's tea and sympathy, I resolved to visit Kitty after all.

I approached the Manor House with more confidence this time. It was fast becoming part of my territory. The tulips in the tubs standing sentry either side of the front door had opened up since my first visit, revealing petals the colour of Sicilian lemons. They reminded me of my aunt's travels to Dutch bulb fields and Mediterranean citrus groves.

Heartened by the thought of Auntie May and her affection for Kitty and Bunny, I raised the door knocker and gave several sharp raps. A moment later, the door was flung wide with such energy and enthusiasm that I could hardly believe it was Kitty on the other side. She flashed a huge, warm smile that I'd never seen on her before. It made her look like a different person.

"Hello, Sophie," she beamed. "That's good timing. I've just been enjoying some cakes fresh from the oven. Will you join me?"

I couldn't help but smile in return. "Thank you, I'd love to. You're looking very well, by the way."

She beamed. "The restorative power of unbroken sleep. I've been running on empty for years. I didn't realise the effects of sleep deprivation until Hector recommended a book about sleep. He's very good, your Hector. I slept like the dead last night, knowing I wouldn't have to keep getting up and down for Mother. I feel like a new mother whose baby's just slept through the night for the first time."

The transformation was certainly remarkable. Not only did she look happier, healthier and younger, she was also speaking much more coherently. I resolved to start getting in some early nights myself, without Hector.

As we padded through to the kitchen, I noticed the bundles of newspapers that had lined the corridor had disappeared. She waved a hand as we passed the radiator, against which now lay a series of cardboard boxes lined with old blankets, each holding at least one sleeping cat.

"As you can see, I've been having a declutter while Mother's not here to prevent me doing it. Goodness knows what she wanted with all those papers, but she'll have to live without them now. I've got so much time on my hands without Mother to look after, and Billy said I should make the most of it and do something useful. He's been helping me. He set up all those boxes. They'll help keep the wretched cats out from under my feet."

The kitchen was also transformed, the surfaces clean and fragrant with pine disinfectant, and the windows were spotless. Even the table was clear, bar a wire mesh cooling rack. A batch of chocolate brownies formed a neat three-by-four array of military neatness, apart from one that Kitty had already eaten. They looked irresistible.

Kitty filled the kettle from the cold tap and set it to boil, then fetched what looked like her best china from a glass-fronted display cabinet at the far end of the room and a jug of milk from the fridge.

"I haven't baked for ages," she said cheerfully, putting a paper doily on a large plate and arranging the brownies to radiate out from the centre like petals.

"It looks like you're good at it." I wanted to encourage her, not least because it seemed to be making her so happy. I wondered whether we could find room for some of her baking at the shop without upsetting Mrs Wetherley, our usual supplier. No doubt Kitty would welcome the little income it might bring her, and having an outside interest would do her good.

"I can't get over how well you're looking. What a transformation. Not that you didn't look lovely before, of course."

Fortunately she didn't mind my backhanded compliment and held up the plate to offer me a brownie.

"I believe sleep deprivation is used as a form of torture in some countries," I said, having read the blurb on the sleep book in the shop.

I bit into my cake. It was as delicious as it looked.

"Very effective it would be, too," she said, her mouth full of her second brownie. "Trouble is, Mother sleeps badly and needs help with everything these days, so if she wakes in the night needing the loo, she wakes me too. Her sleeping pills help her a little, but not much."

I watched Kitty fill my teacup with a steady hand.

"What a good thing you don't take sleeping pills, so you always hear when she needs you."

She grimaced. "I can't say I haven't been tempted, but there's a strong disincentive. If I don't get up to help her in the night, I pay for it in the morning with extra laundry duties. It's only since she's been in hospital that I've had time to read the book about sleep. Now I've discovered

155

all sorts of ways to improve her quality of sleep, as well as mine. Sleep hygiene, they call it. Funny sort of term, don't you think?"

"A hot bath before bed makes me sleep better."

"That's one of the recommendations, funnily enough. What sort of bubble bath do you like?"

This intimacy was growing quickly now. I felt we were regressing to teenagers. Any minute now, we'd be styling each other's hair and painting our toenails.

"Rose, or anything else floral," I replied.

I finished the last bite of my brownie and remembered my mission.

"By the way, Kitty, I hope you weren't upset by me and Paul arguing on your doorstep just now. I didn't mean to get into a row with him."

She waved a hand dismissively. "No-one ever does. He's just like that. Stuart's the same. Argumentative buggers, the pair of them. Mother says they take after their father. In everything except looks, of course." She indicated her face. "We all take after Mother in appearance. There are seven of us, you know. She had ten children by three fathers. Three by her first husband have died already. I was my father's only child." She beamed again. "He doted on me, which of course wound the rest of them up no end."

I could imagine. "I've met Paul and Stuart. What about the other seven? I heard they'd all moved away."

Her face fell. "Yes, I never see any of them now. Some of them I never got to know in the first place, as they'd grown up and left home before I was old enough to remember much about them. Three of them are already dead."

"So awful when a child dies before their parents. That goes against nature."

She fixed me with a curious stare. "Do you have children, Sophie?"

I shook my head. "I'm only twenty-five. Twenty-six next month."

She raised her eyebrows. "If you'd started when my mother did, you would have a nine-year-old by now. Too late for me, though. I've let my mother down by not providing any grandchildren. She loves babies. Her grandchildren are all adults now." She reached across the table to squeeze my hand. "Don't you leave it too late, will you?"

I said nothing, and we sat in silence for a moment.

"Do you have brothers and sisters, nieces and nephews?" she asked.

"I'm afraid not."

"Poor you. They're not all bad, you know, siblings. I just wish I was closer to mine. Mother rather screwed things up for me. Edith next door told me Mother didn't handle her transition from husband to husband well."

So Joshua's late wife Edith had been Bunny's friend too.

"Edith said Mother always made such a fuss of her latest husband that the children from the previous marriage resented their father's successor." She shrugged. "But she'd have been silly not to prefer the living one over the dead. She favoured the new husband's children too." She refilled our teacups and pressed me to take a second brownie. "So on balance, I'm rather glad she stopped when she got to me."

She gave a wry smile. Catching up with her sleep, even for only a few days, had softened her complexion. On her, the distinctive long face and aquiline nose of her brothers would once have been extremely pretty.

"Still, when you have such a big family, you can't all expect to get on like a house on fire, can you?" She pointed to the cake plate. "Maybe I should give them some of these next time they visit. Then they might stop by more often."

The thought of Paul and Stuart being won over by a plate of home-made cakes struck me as comical, and when I began to giggle, Kitty did too.

"We'll all be equal in the end," said Kitty, topping up the teapot and spilling a little from the spout on her way back from the kettle. "Ashes to ashes. Tealeaves to dust. At the end of the day, you can't take it with you."

"What, cake?"

We both found my reply so extraordinarily funny that our convulsive giggles brought Billy in from the back garden, stamping loose soil off his Wellingtons on to the doormat.

"What's got into you two?"

Kitty calmed down enough to fetch another cup and pour him some tea.

"Oh, this and that. Families. Life. Death. Wills."

The word wills brought me to my senses, or at least nudged me in their general direction.

"Wills?" Billy came to join us at the table. This time there was no need to tip a cat off a chair before sitting down. "What, like where there's a will there's a way?"

Kitty gave the top of Billy's head a playful slap as she set a teacup in front of him. "No, you dunce, like Mother's will. I know she's got one, but I've never seen it. She never asked me to sign it."

Billy stirred three teaspoons of sugar into his tea.

"That probably just means you're a beneficiary. You can't be a witness to a will if you stand to gain by it."

"Really? You think she'll leave me the house? Or at least some money? I'm not so sure after all I put her through in my younger days." She sobered up a little.

I thought another joke might cheer her up. "She didn't ask me to sign it either, so she must be leaving something to me too."

As Kitty and I folded up into giggles again, Billy remained stern.

"I don't know what you're so amused about, Kitty Carter. For all you know, she could be leaving everything to the cats' home."

With that cold water cast upon our mirth, we quietened down a little. Then Kitty took a big gulp of tea and brightened. "Oh well, who cares. If she leaves it all to the cats' home, I'll just opt for that old Indian custom, suttee. Like Mrs Aouda in *Around the World in Eighty Days*. You know about her, don't you, Sophie? Your aunt wrote a famous book about suttee, campaigning against it. I'll just throw myself on Mother's funeral pyre. I always have liked a nice toasty bonfire."

Kitty and I creased up in laughter at the thought, while Billy picked up the phone and called Hector to come and take me home.

"But I only live two doors away," I objected as Hector took my arm to lead me out of Kitty's kitchen. "You've got a bad memory."

"Thank you, Billy." Hector's voice was stern. "Kitty."

"Kitty's been telling me all about that lovely sleep book—" I began, but forgot what I was going to say.

Billy winked at Hector. "She's all yours, boy."

As Hector led me down the passage to the front door, Kitty was trying to stuff the remaining brownies into a

159

cake tin, while Billy wrestled as many as he could from her and put them in the bin.

"Whatever you do, Bill, don't put them out for the birds," Hector called over his shoulder as he closed the front door behind us.

27 Council of War

My eyes still closed, despite the sunshine streaming in through the bedroom curtains, I reached one arm across the duvet to check for any signs of life. Yes, Hector had stayed the night again, but Blossom was nowhere to be seen. The door was closed. He must have shut the poor little thing out of the bedroom for the night. I opened my mouth to protest, then put my hands to my temple.

"Do you know, I think there was something funny about Kitty's brownies?"

"You don't say." He reached over to stroke my cheek, and I opened my eyes just as he sat up and swung his legs on to the floor. "You mean you've guessed her secret herbal ingredient? And I'm not talking about catnip." But there his sympathy ended. "Come on, look lively, or you'll be late for work."

I groaned. "Oh no, is it a weekday? I think I've got food poisoning."

He said nothing but ran lightly down the stairs. Hearing the comforting sound of the kettle being filled for breakfast, I went down to join him, at a rather slower pace.

"Still, at least the experience wasn't wasted," I said, trying to sound cheerier than I felt as he handed me a slice of buttered toast.

"Wasted is the word." Hector was doing his best to look disapproving but not making a very good job of it.

"I found out that Kitty has no idea who will inherit from Bunny. She thinks she might be left destitute. Which is sad, but she's putting a remarkably brave face on it."

I was glad to have diverted Hector from my embarrassment.

"So who does she think might be in the running?"

I shrugged. "She seemed a bit vague about the whole thing. I think Bunny gets some kind of satisfaction out of keeping them all guessing. But it's backfired, because they all seem at odds with each other, and with Bunny too."

"Maybe they'll all assassinate each other in a race to inherit." He held his teaspoon in the air to presage a declaration. "And then there were nine."

"Six, actually," I said through a mouthful of the best toast I had ever tasted. "Three are already dead."

"He looks officious," said Hector as we left my cottage for work.

We stopped half way down the path, and I followed Hector's gaze. A suited man was just getting out of an unmarked white van outside the Manor House.

"It's hard not to look officious when you're carrying a clipboard, but he looks the type who'd seem officious in his pyjamas."

We lingered by my front gate watching the man pat Bunny's gatepost as if testing its strength, before pulling out a tape measure to check the height of the tiny step from pavement to path.

"Maybe he's an estate agent valuing the house for sale," said Hector. "He seems very thorough."

"You don't think he's one of Paul's men starting work on the place already? Talk about jumping the gun!"

Another man in a suit emerged from the driver's side of the van, wielding a large camera with a fancy lens.

"Perhaps we should ask?" I said. "Or at least check their credentials? They could be tricksters, about to swindle Kitty out of lots of money for tarmacking her drive or replacing a missing roof tile."

"They certainly don't look like Paul's men. I've seen them in action at The Bluebird. A couple of his workers were leaving the pub after work yesterday, and I've never seen anyone wearing so many copies of the same logo in my life. Even their tools were branded, and his vans are liveried too. I know publicity is helpful for winning new business, but his is completely over the top."

I chewed my lip. "Maybe he's making a point about his surname, having been traumatised by his mother's speedy remarriage when he was a little boy, without giving him time to grieve for his late father. Her abandoning his surname might feel like a betrayal – a partial abandonment of himself."

"You've been spending too much time in our psychology section, Sophie." Hector, as ever, had a more practical interpretation of events. "He might just be worried about people pinching his stuff. Or about his staff misbehaving behind his back. If they're all wearing company t-shirts, they'll never get away with any mischief. Perhaps I should do the same for my shop staff." He patted my bottom to move me along and turned in the direction of the strangers. "Come on, there's only one way to find out."

Refusing to be herded like cattle, I stayed where I was and let him address the strangers without me.

"As a friend of the householder, might I ask what you're doing here?" he said to the officious looking man.

"You can ask," replied the man, writing something on his clipboard.

"Council inspectors," said the driver, coming to join them.

"Inspecting what, exactly?"

The two strangers exchanged glances. "There's a limit to what I can tell you. What exactly is your relationship to the householder here?"

"I'm the owner's great-nephew," said Hector, so stoutly that even I almost believed him.

"Then I can advise you we have been despatched to check the suitability of her property prior to her discharge from hospital."

"Will you be going inside?"

"Of course."

"Have you made an appointment?"

"With Mrs Carter?"

"With her daughter Kitty, who is also her carer."

"We were told she lived alone."

"Then you were told wrong. Who by?"

"By her daughter." The man looked at his clipboard. "A Mrs Lot."

"I don't think so."

The council inspector shrugged. Meanwhile, his colleague produced some kind of laser device with which he appeared to check the gradient of the slope from front gate to porch.

"Well, now you know who we are, you're welcome to discuss any further problems or queries with the hospital."

"Thank you, I shall."

Hector turned abruptly and marched back to my gate. I could tell from his brisk walk that he was not best pleased. I hastened my pace to keep up with him.

"That Mrs Lot is nothing but trouble," he said. "I'm going to phone the council when we get to the shop and grass her up as a fraud."

"Don't forget you also claimed to be Bunny's relative," I reminded him, and he frowned.

When we reached the bookshop, Hector immediately became immersed in a meeting with a visiting rep from a travel guide company eager to install a branded display unit, so I decided to phone the hospital myself.

"And you are?" asked the nurse pleasantly.

"Mrs Carter's great-nephew's other half." I spoke quickly before my nerve could fail me. I don't know what it was about this case that was turning us all into serial liars. Fortunately, the nurse seemed to be the one that Hector had chatted up the previous Sunday.

"Oh yes, we met last weekend, didn't we? Your husband was the handsome one with curly dark hair and green eyes."

Her calling him my husband gave me a little thrill, although I doubted she remembered the colour of all her patients' visitors' eyes.

"We met some people outside her house this morning claiming to be council workers checking her house was safe for her to return to before she could be discharged," I explained. "They had what looked like official council badges, but as a precaution we wanted to check with you."

The nurse didn't seem to mind. "I'm so sorry, I think we presumed your – your aunt, is it? – would have passed the message on."

"My aunt?" For a moment I imagined a ghostly May had dropped by.

"Yes, you know, the aunt who was visiting at the same time as you, the one who brought so many gifts. A Mrs Loft, was it?"

I could hear the smile in her voice. Perhaps Bunny had given her some of Mrs Lot's chocolates.

"Oh yes, of course. Dear Aunt Petunia." I almost gagged as I said it. She was no more related to Bunny than I was.

"Your Aunt Petunia told me she'd requested the council inspection. She was worried that Mrs Carter might have mobility difficulties on her return."

She paused as if expecting me to say something, but as I was dumbstruck by Mrs Lot's interference, the nurse continued in a kindly tone.

"There are all sorts of home improvement grants, for things like handrails and toilet seat boosters, available that might help her. She should get what she can."

"I'm sure that is precisely my aunt's intention."

Aunt Petunia, that is.

28 Room to Let

No sooner had I finished serving morning coffee to the school-run mums than an expensively dressed woman of middle-age came in and headed straight for the trade counter without a glance at the rest of the shop. Well-groomed and in full make-up, she was clearly not part of the primary school drop-off set. Hector, scanning in new sample stock left by a visiting rep, put down the scanner and gave her his full attention.

"Do you carry ads?" She glanced around the shop in search of a bit of wall space that wasn't obscured by bookshelves. There wasn't much. "I mean, do you have a noticeboard for local advertisements?" She pulled a neatly written pink index card from her designer handbag and thrust it at Hector. He read the details.

"You're after a lodger?"

She nodded.

"I'm afraid we only carry posters for village events." He pointed to the noticeboard behind the door, already covered with bus timetables, adverts for local community group meetings and the month's church service schedule. "The village shop has more space than we do for this kind of thing. Carol charges for putting up notices, but only fifty pence a week. Wouldn't you be better off posting something online? Especially as your property is in Slate Green rather than Wendlebury. You'll reach a much wider audience via the internet. Or do you have a particular reason for advertising here?"

She took the card back. "Maybe. I don't suppose you happen to know anyone in the village who's looking for accommodation, do you?"

Intrigued, I wandered over from the tearoom to join them. "I heard in the pub the other day that a local builder's about to leave his wife. He might be looking for a temporary place."

Her icy stare suggested I'd just stabbed her in the heart. "Do you mean Paul Brady? Very funny. That rumour would be wrong, then. I suppose the next thing you'll be telling me is that you're his bit of stuff."

As she ran her cold eyes up and down my body, I took a couple of steps back.

Hector came to my rescue. "No, she's my bit of stuff, actually." It was my turn to glare. "But yes, she does mean Paul Brady. I take it you're Mrs Brady?"

"Mrs Fenella Brady. And the thing is—"

She looked over at the tearoom to make sure the customers weren't eavesdropping. Having fallen silent as they tuned in to our conversation, they immediately began chattering self-consciously.

Fenella lowered her voice, perhaps realising she was making a fool of herself. "I'm sorry, that was a stupid remark. I apologise unreservedly. I don't really think he's having an affair, I'm just tense right now."

Hector nudged me.

"I'm sorry too, it was wrong of me to gossip about someone I hardly know," I said, inwardly cursing Donald for putting the idea in my head.

Fenella and I smiled awkwardly at each other for a moment, before she began again.

"The thing is, with my son away at university, the house seems so empty, and my husband's always out working. He hardly even comes home for meals these days. I never see him. God knows what he's up to. It's a huge house to spend so much time in by myself. I thought having a lodger might be rather fun. And I thought I might get a more pleasant type of person from a village than from town."

Hector's golden rule was to be helpful to all customers, no matter how irritating or embarrassing.

"What sort of lodger are you looking for?" I asked. "A student, perhaps?"

She wrinkled her nose. "No, I'd rather have someone more grown-up and sophisticated. Someone who would be good company during the lonely evenings at home." She glanced coquettishly at Hector, who gave a nervous cough. "I thought perhaps a nice executive who lives some distance away but needs a pied-a-terre for local work. Having someone else in the house would make me feel more secure at night when Paul's out late, now that Dominic's away in term-time. He's a pharmacy student, you know. He's a clever boy."

"Try asking the human resources departments of big local employers. If they're regularly putting up visitors in hotels, they could well be interested. If you work directly with them, you won't have to pay commission to a middleman for the booking."

Fenella's face relaxed a little.

"What a good idea. Thank you. You're very kind." She glanced across to the tearoom again. "Your coffee smells good. I think I'll stop for one, if that's OK?"

I led her to the one free table and pulled out a chair for her. She sat down heavily and plonked her fancy handbag on the other chair.

"God knows, I shouldn't be indulging myself this way. Dom's university pharmacy studies won't pay for themselves. That's another reason for having a lodger – it would give me a bit of spare cash for treats. I'm afraid my husband is so tied up with his business that he doesn't realise how much it costs to run a household these days. Or doesn't want to know. He takes after his mother." She sighed. "Her excuse for not sponsoring Dom's fees is that she doesn't hold with drugs, which is nonsense. At her age, she must be held together by them. Poor boy will be saddled with a student loan for decades."

If she was after a free coffee, she was barking up the wrong waitress.

"Did you see her jewellery?"

I'd had to wait till the shop was finally empty of customers to put this question to Hector. He shook his head.

"If she simply took off all her jewellery and threw it on the table, there'd be the equivalent to the price of a car." Hector was unmoved. "Enough money to buy a brand-new Land Rover."

That caught his attention.

"I notice she didn't buy a book to thank us for being helpful," he said. "If she's bored at home, what she needs is a good book. You're never lonely with a good book. And our advice was worth more than the price of her coffee."

He powered down his laptop and closed the lid. "If she's going to go round slagging off Bunny in public, she's no friend of mine."

"Maybe she's hoping Bunny will leave everything to her precious Dominic in her will? What's he like?"

Hector pulled out the cash drawer to tot up the day's takings a little earlier than usual. "I've no idea. I don't think I've ever set eyes on him. Paul brings his family back to the village on Show Day, as most people with any Wendlebury connections do, so I suppose I might recognise him if I saw him, especially if he takes after his father's side in looks. He will have grown up in Slate Green, where they live now. Which makes me wonder why Fenella is going round Wendlebury looking for a lodger."

He started stacking pound coins in piles of ten.

"Wendlebury's hardly an industrial zone. Carol, Donald and I are the only local employers besides the farmers and a smattering of self-employed working from home. Nearly all the villagers are families, rather than singletons looking for lodgings."

"Maybe she isn't looking for a lodger at all, and that was just an excuse to check that Paul really has got a building contract up here. She might suspect he's carrying on with some woman, hence that hideous 'bit of stuff' remark. If her suspicions proved right, she might be planning to seek revenge by spreading rumours about his character throughout the village."

Hector thumbed through the banknotes. "Remind me not to ditch you any time soon, Sophie. You have far too many good ideas for a woman scorned."

I grinned. It might not be the best reassurance that he wasn't about to abandon me for Becky or the Battersby rep, but it was better than nothing.

"Do you think Fenella might have something to do with Bunny's abduction?"

Hector looked askance. "I'm not sure she'd have the physical strength, nor the gumption. She's quite slight, and she didn't seem exactly resourceful."

"No, but if she's got a hulking spoiled son in his prime, bright enough to study pharmacy, he'll have brains as well as the brute strength of a young man."

"But would anyone really be so keen to avoid student debt that they'd murder their granny?"

"It would explain why Bunny didn't resist her abductor. She'd have recognised him and been glad to see him."

"Wouldn't she think it odd that he'd appeared at the crack of dawn, presumably in her bedroom?"

I shook my head. "If Bunny sleeps as badly as Kitty claims, she might not have realised how early it was. Old people's body clocks are different to ours. Fenella, being her daughter-in-law, would probably have had a front-door key to the Manor House. Not that she'd have needed one, as the lock is jammed open. Plus Dominic, as a pharmacy student, would have professional knowledge of which drugs to administer to knock Bunny and Kitty out." I pictured Fenella's manicured hands with their flashy rings and bracelets gently pushing open that big front door. "And I tell you what else: Fenella would be just the sort of person to have a fur coat."

29 The Penniless Mile

"Ah, Sophie, there you are!"

Shortly before closing time, the vicar cornered me in the tearoom. I'd been avoiding him since Sunday, as he wanted to prepare me for teaching the Sunday School. I retreated behind the counter and pretended to be busy stacking teacups and saucers.

"Hello, vicar!" I tried to make my voice sound more relaxed than I felt, without encouraging him to linger. "I'm afraid I can't offer you your usual mocha as I've just turned the coffee machine off for the night."

"No problem, I've just had a cup of tea at home. What I'm actually after is you."

Much as I feared. "The thing is—" I was about to launch into an apology for avoiding him, but he interrupted, clearly on a mission.

"I just wondered whether you'd like to accompany me to visit Bunny Carter in hospital? My wife's away at her sister's, and I thought a woman's touch might be welcome. You know, taking in clean underwear, and the like."

He coughed, a little embarrassed. I grinned. Unlike the vicar, Bunny seemed pretty unembarrassable.

173

"I'd love to," I said, glad to have the excuse to visit her again. "We can call in at the Manor House on the way to collect anything Kitty thinks she might need. Can we go via the village shop so I can buy Bunny a newspaper and some chocolates?"

"Of course. How kind of you."

"You can slope off a bit early if you like, Sophie," said Hector. "It's very quiet."

"Thanks. Shall I come and see you when I get back to tell you how she is?"

"If you like. Or just give me a ring or text me if you're too tired. Otherwise, I'll see you in the morning."

I turned off the lights above the counter and put up the 'Sorry, Tea's Off' sign. Grabbing my jacket from its hook, I was just about to leave when the door swung open and in strolled Becky without her usual accessory, baby Arthur. She flashed a radiant smile, which was probably meant exclusively for Hector.

Hector smiled back and came out from behind the counter to follow the vicar and me to the door. "Give Bunny my love," he said, flipping the "Open" sign to "Closed" a full fifteen minutes before our official closing time.

The vicar sensed my disquiet and sought to distract me as we got in his car.

"The journey will give us the opportunity for a chat about our plans for Sunday School."

My heart sank.

"By the way, Kate's said she'll help you with the first few sessions till you're comfortable running it on your own. Kate used to lead it before she retired, and only gave it up when she went on her long holiday to Australia last year."

Kate was Hector's godmother, a zesty, upbeat lady whom I liked very much. Suddenly the prospect of teaching Sunday School didn't seem as daunting.

The vicar pulled up by the shop, and we went inside. I hoped the vicar wouldn't disapprove of liqueur chocolates.

I should have known better. "Yum!" He eyed the packet. "They'll be a better tonic than any medicine." I grabbed a second pack for us to share in the car, after reading the label to check the alcohol content wasn't enough to put the vicar over the legal limit for driving.

I was just getting the right money out of my purse when a woman not much older than myself entered the shop and came to stand beside me at the counter.

"Excuse me, can you please tell me where Mrs Brady lives?"

"Mrs Brady?" Carol hesitated, glancing at the vicar for guidance. "There's no Mrs Brady in this village. The Brady boys moved away a long time ago, taking their wives with them."

The woman turned to me. "Do you know a Mrs Brady? She'd be very old."

"Mrs Brady, old lady?" I said before I could stop myself. "Oh, that Mrs Brady. If it's who I think you mean, she's not Mrs Brady any more. She's Mrs Carter now."

"How odd that Stuart never told me his mother had married again." The woman's face softened as she mentioned him. "How adorable to find love again at her age. Like mother, like son, even though they've been estranged for so long. Isn't it sad that I've never met my own mother-in-law? It's not as if we live a million miles away. It's only the Midlands." She fluttered her eyelashes at the vicar. "I'm always telling Stuart that he ought to make up his differences with his mother before it's too late. I guess that's why he dashed down here when she was rushed to hospital."

The vicar gave a nervous smile.

The woman turned back to me. "Could you tell me where Mrs Carter lives, please? Stuart told me he'd most likely stop at her house while he was visiting, but he forgot to tell me her address or which hospital she's in, and I need to find him urgently to tell him some very good news."

"Why don't you phone him or text him first to check?" Her side of the story was sounding odd, and I thought he might prefer to be alerted to her imminent arrival.

"My news for him is far too exciting to tell him over the phone." Her hands went to her flat stomach. You didn't have to be psychic to guess what her news might be. The old dog! Stuart was old enough to be her father, never mind the baby's.

For a moment, none of us spoke. If she didn't know about Bunny's third marriage, she might not know about Kitty either.

The vicar took charge. "My dear, by a lucky coincidence, Sophie and I are just about to call in at the Manor House to collect some personal effects to take to Mrs Carter in hospital. As far as I know, Stuart won't be there at present, but I can introduce you to his half-sister Kitty."

"I'm sure she'll be very interested to meet you," added Carol, with an air of mischief.

The vicar turned to me. "Sophie, I know you had something you needed to discuss with Carol. Why don't you stay here to catch up with her, while I introduce this lady to Kitty and fetch Bunny's things from the Manor House? I'll come back to collect you shortly."

I didn't have something I needed to discuss with Carol, but I realised he was just being discreet.

"Righto, vicar."

With that, he ushered the woman out of the shop and into his car, leaving Carol and me staring after them as they drove off down the High Street.

I turned to Carol. "Why has Stuart told her he's staying at the Manor House? The hospital's closer to Slate Green, where he lives, than it is to here. So what was all that about coming down from the Midlands?"

Carol bit her lip. "You've never met Stuart's wife before, have you?"

"No."

"I was at school with her."

"Really? I don't want to seem rude, Carol, but that lady seemed about half your age."

Carol nodded, wide-eyed. "Exactly. If you ask me, it looks like a case of botany."

I bit my lip to suppress a smile. "I think the word you're looking for is bigamy, Carol."

Like mother, like son, indeed.

"I'm afraid I've left both of them in a rather awkward situation," said the vicar. "But all credit to Kitty. She made Angelica welcome. She seemed more intrigued than disturbed by evidence of her brother's second wife. At least we've kept Angelica away from Bunny's bedside. We don't want to upset Bunny further while she's unwell."

"I think we'd better not tell her about Angelica, even though she'll be glad to hear a new grandchild is on the way," I said as we turned from the High Street on to the main road and headed towards Slate Green.

"Do you think we should phone Stuart to warn him?" I didn't want to make matters any worse for any of the parties involved, including his first wife.

"I don't have his number, as he's not one of my parishioners. Nor do I know his postal address. Do you?" He flicked his indicator to follow the diversion around the closed bridge.

"Afraid not. I've only met him once. He came into Hector's House the other night asking me to change a fifty-pound note into pound coins. I didn't trust him, to be honest. There was something odd about him. When I asked why he needed so many pound coins, he said he wanted to donate it to your penny mile."

"My penny mile? What penny mile?"

I gave a triumphant laugh. "I knew he was fibbing! What's more, as he left the shop, his trouser pockets were jangling as if they were already full of change."

"Maybe he'd just raided young Angelica's piggybank." The vicar clapped one hand over his mouth. "Oh, I'm sorry, Sophie, that remark was unworthy of a clergyman. Pretend you didn't hear it. I'm a wicked, wicked man."

I laughed. "It must be hard to be virtuous all the time."

He grinned. "Is it, Sophie? You tell me."

178

30 A Real Tonic

Bunny was noticeably cheerier and more energetic now, although her bruises were more spectacular. She reminded me of a Polaroid photo, slowly developing its colours before your very eyes.

Mr Murray asked whether there was anything she wanted from the hospital shop, then pottered off to fetch us coffee from the vending machine, leaving us alone to chat.

"So, my dear, how is the lovely Hector?"

I couldn't help but smile.

"He's fine, thank you, and he sends you his love."

She pressed her hand against her heart.

"That's worth having, as I'm sure you know. He is a dear boy, and you are lucky to have him. And he you, of course."

My eyes suddenly filled with tears. "You think so?" A tear escaped and rolled down my cheek. I reached up to brush it away, hoping she wouldn't notice, but she was too quick for me.

"Oh, my dear, have you had a lovers' tiff?"

Her smile was so kind that I couldn't help but spill out my worries. With three husbands behind her, and goodness knows how many boyfriends, she had considerably more experience of love than I did.

I spoke quickly, knowing that the vicar would not be gone long. "I'm probably just being silly, but when the vicar and I left the shop tonight, this beautiful girl Becky arrived, and he seemed very pleased to see her."

"Carol's daughter, Becky?"

I nodded.

"Hector told me all about Becky when she first moved in with Carol before Christmas. He said she's very well-read. It's only natural that a girl like that would visit your bookshop. Are you saying you don't welcome her custom?"

I bit my lip. "The thing is, she doesn't just come to buy books. I found out the other day that he's been asking her to help in the shop when I'm not there. And when Mr Murray and I left the shop just now, as she was arriving, Hector let her in and immediately turned the door sign to 'Closed'."

Bunny reached out to clasp both my hands. Hers were thin and bony and smooth as silk. "It must have been about closing time anyway?"

I sniffed. "Not for another fifteen minutes."

"I don't think that's any cause for alarm."

"But that's not the only thing." I wondered how much I should tell her. This visit was meant to cheer her up, not weigh her down with my own woes. "He's started chatting up other women too, like one of the nurses here the other day. When I first met him, he seemed much more reserved."

Bunny held up a hand to silence me. "Nonsense. Hector loves you. He's been telling me all about you since you first moved to the village, yet he has barely said a word about Becky lately, nor any other woman, bar his dear mother."

She leaned forward, a twinkle in her eyes. "Maybe there's another reason for the change in him. You've restored his self-confidence. You've made him feel attractive as a man, and he's rather enjoying the effect you have on him. That's a powerful tool in a relationship. Trust me, I should know."

She sat back again, more comfortable this time when her back touched the pillows. "Mind you, I've been reading about toy boys in those awful magazines they keep in the patients' lounge. If I was going to choose one, I could do worse than pick Hector. A young stallion of a man! If you tire of him, just send him down to me at the Manor House."

I couldn't help laughing. Much as I loved him, stallion was overstating the case. Still, the only other man she'd seen much of lately was Billy, and he was more of a Shetland pony.

It was probably just as well that the vicar returned at that point, spilling coffee from three flimsy plastic cups squeezed between his hands in a precarious triangle. I helped him set the coffee safely on the bedside locker.

"What are you two giggling about?" He smiled as he settled down into an armchair beside the bed.

"Just girl talk," said Bunny, winking at me. "Nothing of any consequence."

I hoped she was right.

31 Dirty Laundry

By the time the vicar dropped me home, it was dark. I was anxious to check up on Blossom, as it was the longest he'd been alone in the house. Dumping Bunny's bag of laundry in the hall, I decided to take it round to the Manor House in the morning on my way to work.

I'd half-expected Blossom to come running up to greet me, but the cottage was eerily quiet. I went from room to room, turning on lights and calling his name, before finding him curled up like a baby hedgehog, asleep on the bathmat. Scooping him up with one hand, I carried him through to my bedroom, sat on the bed with him on my lap and settled down to call Hector. A text wouldn't tell me whether or not he was alone.

"Your round, boy!" were the first words I heard when he accepted my call. Billy was apparently closer to the mouthpiece than Hector.

"First things first." That was Hector to Billy. "Hello, sweetheart, how's Bunny?"

"On good form. She sends you her love." I didn't elaborate. "Are you at the pub?"

"Got it in one. I just popped over for a quick half after shutting up shop and got buttonholed by Billy."

With or without Becky? I wanted to ask, but didn't want to bring her into the conversation. "Shouldn't he be at the Manor House?"

"He's escaped. Kitty gave him time off for good behaviour. What's this I hear about the vicar delivering some long-lost relative up to the Manor House? I can't get much sense out of Billy about her."

Another voice drowned him out, an uncomfortably familiar one: Paul. "I'll get these, Bill. Hector can catch up afterwards."

I lowered my voice so only Hector might hear. "Her name's Angelica. She's Stuart's wife. Or so she claims. Not the one in Slate Green, but another one. And she's pregnant and he doesn't know it yet."

"Pregnant?" The background noise disappeared, then I heard Hector, slightly muffled, say "No, not Sophie." As the hubbub resumed around him, he continued, "Billy's left her having a heart-to-heart with Kitty. Are you coming up to join us?"

"Do you want me to?"

"Of course I do. But you don't have to. Would it help persuade you if I told you Paul seems bent on buying everyone drinks?"

I ran my free hand gently over Blossom's powder puff of a back. He began to purr in his sleep.

"Quite the opposite. Besides, it sounds like a boys' night out." That gave him the chance to confess if Becky was with him, but he didn't. "I'm going to put my feet up with Blossom and have an early night. You're welcome to come to mine later if you like."

"Thanks all the same, but I'll give it a miss. I'll wait and see you bright-eyed and bushy-tailed in the morning." I heard the unmistakeable chink of a round of

184

beer glasses being set down on the table in front of him. "Though I'm not sure I will be at this rate."

As I clicked "end call", I had a horrible feeling that if it wasn't Becky luring him away, then Blossom's presence in my cottage might have put him off staying here. I hoped I hadn't made a dreadful mistake in taking Blossom on.

As I reached across the pillow to turn my alarm off at eight o'clock, my hand brushed against Blossom's soft fur. I was tempted to snuggle down with him for ten more minutes, then I remembered I had to drop off at the Manor House a bag of Bunny's dirty laundry.

I drew back the bedroom curtains, blinking against the spring sunshine. Working on a Saturday wasn't really so bad now I'd got used to it. If I didn't have to be at the shop by nine, I'd have slept through this glorious morning.

Plenty of other people were already out and about enjoying the weather. A young girl was strolling up towards the shop with a scruffy grey dog on a lead, and Dr Perkins was just striding past my house in the opposite direction. I watched him pause to exchange a cheery greeting with Joshua, who, always up with the lark, was busy deadheading daffodils in his front garden.

Then I remembered I was still in my nightie, and I stepped back from the window before anyone might spot me. I scrambled into my clothes, downed a yoghurt for breakfast, fed Blossom and grabbed the laundry bag before heading out of the front door.

I waved to Joshua who was looking through his front room window as I passed his gate, swinging the laundry bag as I walked. I was glad to have this excuse to visit Kitty again so soon, to find out what she'd made of

Angelica, and to try to detect whether Stuart really was guilty of bigamy. If so, no wonder he was broke, even without throwing his money away on slot machines.

I was feeling much more positive after a good night's sleep. Blossom, who slept almost constantly, was a good influence. But my contentment was to be cut short in an unimaginably cruel way.

The door to the Manor House was ajar again. Either I wasn't the first visitor this morning, or Billy still hadn't fixed the faulty catch. I knocked on the door. The eerie quiet within filled me with unease. Why was no-one up and about? Perhaps Billy would be slow to emerge after the previous night's shenanigans with Paul, Hector and friends, but not Kitty.

Pushing the door open and tiptoeing inside, I decided to empty Bunny's laundry into the basket in the utility room, so that Kitty wouldn't mistake the black bag for rubbish and put it in the wheelie bin. It irked me that the hospital had put Bunny's laundry in a bin bag. It seemed disrespectful.

Early morning sun streamed in through the large picture window in the utility room, and the heat made Bunny's laundry smell nauseating. As I opened the window for some fresh air, a strangled cry of my name came from the garden. There, just beyond the terrace, stood Billy, staring at me in horror as if he thought I was a ghost. His hangover must have been a corker. I hoped Hector's wasn't as bad.

"Morning, Billy," I called cheerily, hardening my heart against his self-inflicted misery.

When he didn't return my greeting, I went outside, assuming he might not be able to hear me from the garden. As I descended the steps from the terrace, I realised his anguish had nothing to do with a hangover.

There at his feet in a crumpled heap lay Kitty, a dark pool haloing her head. Dangling in Billy's left hand was a large black-handled hammer, its silver claw darkened with tacky blood.

"It wasn't me, Sophie, honest to God, it wasn't me. I found her like this just now. I only left the house for a few minutes after I got up this morning to fetch some sausages from the village shop for another breakfast fry-up, like she asked."

I stepped back, my hand over my mouth, before kneeling down beside her prone body to check for signs of life. I did not want to believe that she was gone, though her complexion was waxy and her chest still.

"She's definitely passed, my lovely." I wasn't sure whether Billy's term of endearment was aimed at Kitty or me. "I'm so sorry. I know you was getting to be friends with her."

I fought back the tears, looking up at the hammer, hanging perilously close now to my own head.

"Is that the murder weapon?"

"Must have been."

"You shouldn't have touched it, Billy. There'll be fingerprints."

I clasped my arms about me to fight off an instinct to hug poor Kitty, though it was far too late to comfort her. Her face was the calmest I'd ever seen it, younger and more beautiful in death.

Billy dropped the hammer to the ground and covered his face with his hands. "I don't know what to think no more."

I stood up, still gazing at Kitty in disbelief. This ending seemed so cruel, just as she was starting to return to some kind of normal life these last few days.

187

"Are you going to call Dr Perkins?" asked Billy as I pulled my mobile phone from my handbag.

"It's too late for him to be of any use now," I said. "This time I'm going straight to the police."

32 The Blame Game

"It's all my fault." Billy let out a pitiful moan as I poured tea into two chunky mugs on Kitty's draining board. I'd put the kettle on as soon as I'd phoned the police.

"Of course it's not." I stirred a generous spoonful of sugar into each mug and handed one to Billy. He clasped both hands around it for comfort.

"It is. I should never have gone out and left her in the company of a stranger."

I'd forgotten about Angelica. "Oh my goodness, do you think she killed Kitty?"

"If she did, the cops will have no trouble tracing her." He gestured towards a soft pink leather handbag at the opposite end of the table. "I reckon she might still be upstairs. There was a light on in one of the spare bedrooms when I got back from The Bluebird last night. I'm guessing she stayed over."

I set down my mug. "Are you sure it was her up there and not an intruder? Why didn't you investigate?"

"Would you take kindly to a drunken old man knocking on your bedroom door at midnight? I wasn't born yesterday. Besides, I had no reason to think it wasn't her. The two of them was getting on like a house

189

on fire when I went up The Bluebird. I thought it was Kitty's lucky day, getting a second new friend in the space of a week. There's not many as will persevere past their first impressions of Kitty, but she's not a bad lass underneath it all. I mean, she wasn't."

He passed his hands over his eyes as if to block out the memory of what he'd just seen. "She was a cracker as a girl, before she got mixed up with all that druggie festival crowd."

"What a waste. And poor Bunny. However are we going to break it to her?"

Just then there was a soft footfall in the hall. One of the cats had woken up and was heading for the back door. I leapt up to block its path, overtaking it on its way to the utility room and locking the cat flap. I didn't want to risk the cats treating Kitty's body like a giant dead mouse. Besides, they might disturb valuable evidence at the crime scene.

A sharp rap at the front door cut short our speculation, followed by a cry of, "Hello!"

I went out to see who it was, hoping it might be the police already, though they'd have had to break the speed limit to reach the village that fast from the Slate Green station, especially with the bridge still closed for repair.

Billy remained slumped over his tea. This morning he seemed so frail. Would he ever dig graves again? I supposed he would have to dig Kitty's.

As I entered the hall, Dr Perkins was walking in without waiting to be invited. I backed up as he came through to the kitchen and dumped his black bag on the table as if he owned the place.

"Sophie, my dear, what on earth are you doing here? Shouldn't you be at work by now?"

I didn't return his too-hearty smile.

"Just doing a quick neighbourly favour on my way to Hector's House. But as it happens, I'm very glad you're here." I turned to Billy. "You stay here and drink your tea. I'll show him." The doctor raised his hands in mock surprise. "Show me what, Sophie?"

I grimaced. "It's Kitty. She's in the garden."

"The garden? Out and about at last? That's good news. What's she doing there?"

"Not much, actually." I hesitated. "You'd better bring your black bag And brace yourself. Although I expect in your line of work you've seen a lot of dead bodies, I don't suppose many of them have been murder victims."

He gave a loud gasp, then followed me outside. As I stopped to make sure the back door was closed to contain the cats, he waited for me to lead him down the terrace steps. When I pointed to where Kitty lay, he put his free hand to his mouth.

"Billy found her," I explained. "And also the hammer that had been used to hit her on the head." Looking at Kitty afresh, I noticed details that had escaped me first time round. Some acid-green leaves were crumpled in her hand. The doctor followed my gaze.

"She must have grabbed the nearest plant to steady herself as she fell," said Dr Perkins. "The wound is at the back of the skull, you'll notice, so the fatal blow must have been delivered from behind. She may not have heard the attacker creep up on her."

The doctor sighed. "I suppose I'd better certify her death." He opened the catch on his bag and pulled out a pad of pre-printed forms which lay conveniently on the top of his medical paraphernalia.

I put my hand on his arm to delay him. "I don't think so, doctor. It's not as if we found her dead in bed of natural causes. Surely this is a matter for the police?

Won't they bring their own doctor along? I've already called them to report this as a suspected murder. They should be here any minute."

He shook his arm to dislodge my hand.

"I'm entirely capable of certifying this lady's cause of death, thank you. You should have called me when you found her."

I resented his patronising attitude. "Like I did when we thought Bunny had been murdered? I've regretted not dialling 999 straight away ever since."

"And didn't you make the right decision? Because, as you well know, Bunny is still very much alive."

"Yes, but Kitty very obviously isn't. This is not a routine medical matter. It's no accident. It's a crime scene – with a crime that only the police can solve."

As the back door creaked open, I spun round, hoping to see the police. But it was only Billy.

"There's nothing for the police to solve here," he said, his face crumpling as he leaned against the door jamb for support. "I tell you, it's all my fault."

33 Billy Pours His Heart Out

We rushed up the steps and ushered him back into the kitchen. I steered him to his seat and settled myself in the next chair, laying my arm around his shoulders to comfort him.

"I should never have left Kitty and go to the pub," he wailed. "I promised Bunny I'd always look out for her if ever she was left on her own."

"And so you did. I've never seen her look as well as she did on Thursday."

He shook his head.

"Sophie, you don't know the half of it. Bunny's natural instinct was to keep her daughter away from temptation and harm. She kept alcohol out of the house so as not to tempt her, even though she used to enjoy a drop herself. She never rumbled the – you know, what Kitty used to grow in the garden."

I doubted his code would fool the doctor.

Billy covered his face with his hands again.

"What she hadn't allowed for was my own addiction. I needed a beer last night, and I abandoned Kitty to her fate. I turned my back on my family duty."

He let his head slump down on to the table, his shoulders heaving as he sobbed in silence.

A flurry of high-heeled footsteps alerted us to Angelica coming downstairs. Seeing us, she hesitated in the kitchen doorway, pale as a sheet of paper. She seemed to realise immediately that she'd walked into a crisis.

"You didn't abandon her," she said, her voice gentle. "Kitty spent the evening with me, remember? We had a good old chat." She crossed the room to lay a comforting hand on Billy's shoulder. "We had a lovely evening. She told me lots of funny stories about what Stuart was like when he was a little boy. Where is Kitty now? Still in bed?"

Her face fell as she interpreted our sombre expressions.

"I'm afraid she's had a terrible accident, Angelica," I said, aware of needing to break bad news gently to someone in her condition. But she seemed already to have sensed what it was.

"You mean my baby will never know his Auntie Kitty?"

She collapsed on to the nearest free dining chair, threw her arms and head down on to the table and began to sob loudly – a little over the top for someone who'd spent only hours in Kitty's company.

"She invited you to stay the night?" asked the doctor. "You mean you've been upstairs since yesterday evening?"

Angelica sat up and wiped her eyes.

"Yes, because she said Stuart was due to be calling in here this morning, so the quickest way for me to get hold of him would be to sit tight and wait."

"So if Stuart wasn't here last night," I asked gently, "where was he?"

Angelica blinked in surprise. "I've no idea. He wasn't answering his mobile phone."

"Didn't that worry you?"

"Oh no, he's always misplacing it or letting it run out of charge. I'm used to him not answering his mobile phone when he's away on business. I gave up worrying about that a long time ago." She flashed a tender smile at the memory of his foibles. "Kitty suggested he might be at their mother's hospital bedside keeping an all-night vigil." Her face fell. "Poor Stuart. Perhaps it will be a double funeral, mother and child together, Bunny and Kitty. How unnatural is that?" Her hands flew protectively to her stomach.

Billy groaned and rubbed his eyes roughly. "Auntie Bunny will outlive the lot of us yet."

"You see, that's exactly why I didn't call the police after Bunny's accident," said Dr Perkins. "She's remarkably resilient. I'm her family doctor, by the way."

He held out his hand for Angelica to shake.

"Former doctor," said Billy, narrowing his eyes. "A retired doctor, not a detective."

"Sherlock Holmes found Dr Watson invaluable," retorted the doctor.

Angelica leapt to Billy's defence.

"Frankly, doctor, if my mother-in-law's injuries put her close enough to death's door to bring Stuart to her bedside to say his goodbyes, I'm wondering whether your response at the scene of her accident was inadequate."

"Thank you, Angelica, my thoughts exactly!" I said, relieved that someone besides me and Hector was seeing sense at last.

"Offering first aid on the spot in a crisis is one thing for those 'Is there a doctor in the house?' moments," she went on. "But trying to be a one-man 999 service is quite another. I hope you wouldn't also try to cover for the fire service?"

"Let's set fire to him and see, shall we?" asked Billy, rallying.

Dr Perkins shot Billy a more venomous look than one might expect from a GP. "My dear lady, if you're looking for suspicious characters, I suggest you look no further than Billy Thompson there."

Billy leapt to his feet so sharply that he knocked over the chair he'd been sitting on. As he clenched his fists, the doctor stepped back to dodge him, and moved the nearest chair between them in self-defence. Billy looked at the chair, thought better of it, and stood up the one he'd knocked over instead.

"After all," the doctor continued, smiling slightly, "Sophie found Billy on the patio with the hammer used to murder Kitty."

"What do you think this is, a board game?" asked Billy, sitting down hard on his chair in astonishment.

"And thinking back to Bunny's 'accident'—" the doctor mimed air quotes at this last word "—Bunny was found in a grave dug by Billy, camouflaged with a grassy tarpaulin, while his means of getting her there, a wheelchair, was clumsily hidden in his compost heap."

"I never touched that wheelchair!" cried Billy.

The doctor hadn't finished. "And who else was a guest of the house when Mrs Lot was found slumped in the driving seat of her car?" His smile slowly broadened and he turned to me, as if hoping to engage my complicity. "Yes, Billy Thompson. I rest my case."

34 A Pauline Conversion

"Nonsense on both counts," I said. "The blood on the hammer was already starting to dry when I found Billy with it. The attack must have happened when he was up at the shop buying sausages. And Billy wasn't at the Manor House at all when Mrs Lot was taken ill."

The doctor blinked. "Wasn't he?"

"He'd been having elevenses at Hector's House during her visit, and found her asleep at the wheel of her car on his way back. As you well know, Dr Perkins, because you happened to be walking past the Manor House when Hector arrived in response to Billy's call to the bookshop."

Angelica looked puzzled. "And Hector is?"

"The local bookseller. He owns the shop where you first met me yesterday."

Angelica raised her eyebrows. "So are booksellers part of the emergency services in this village too? What did you expect Hector to do, fend off her attacker with a copy of *War and Peace*?"

"The police will bag the hammer up and take it away for prints," I said, trying not to panic on Billy's behalf.

"Well, obviously it'll have my fingerprints on it," said Billy crossly. "I picked it up to look at it. It's not as if it's got my name on it."

"Has it got someone else's name on it, then?" asked Angelica.

"I suppose it might have the owner's postcode," I said. "The police are running a campaign at the moment to get people to put postcodes on their valuables in SmartWater. They came in a few weeks ago and did our till."

Billy hesitated. "Funnily enough, there was a name on it, but that don't mean nothing. Anybody could have picked it up from the back of the pub. One of Paul's workmen was telling me last week that they like working out here because they can leave their tools out overnight and no-one will pinch them."

I stared at him. "So whose name is on the hammer?"

Billy cast an apologetic look to Angelica.

"Brady Homes. My cousin Paul Brady's outfit. Estranged half-brother of Kitty and whole brother to this lady's fancy man, Stuart."

"Husband," said Angelica. "Brother to my husband." Then, as if realising she might be positioning herself too close for comfort to the suspect, she added, "Not that I've ever met Paul Brady."

"You haven't missed much," I said before I could stop myself. "I mean, he's rude and abrasive, but that doesn't make him a murderer."

"Some people might even describe him as generous," said Billy. "He buys a good round in the pub."

"Yes, out of self-interest." I hadn't forgiven him yet for hijacking Hector the previous night.

"What self-interest?" asked Angelica

I glanced at Billy.

"It's no secret that he wants to convert this house into a care home for the elderly, against the wishes of Bunny and Kitty."

"Well, I think his plans are laudable," put in the doctor. "Look around you. Can't you see the Manor House would make an excellent care home? Generous room sizes, a beautiful, secluded garden, and a pleasant community setting. As a medical man, I'd give it my seal of approval."

He sounded more like an estate agent than a medic.

"But it is his mother's home, and his sister's," said Billy. "What makes him think he has the right? Why can't he at least hold his horses till his mother passes on? It's not likely to be a long wait at her age, God have mercy on her soul."

"You've just said yourself she'll outlive the lot of us," returned the doctor. "Besides, the pair of them would have had a much better quality of life if properly cared for in a good home. You're all talking nonsense. Paul was well on the way to converting the Manor."

Billy wasn't rising to the bait. "I may not be a medical man. Not even a retired medical man. But I knows about human decency and independence and people's rights. And I'm afraid my cousin Paul's been pushing them too far."

"I notice it doesn't stop you drinking Paul's pints, though," retorted the doctor. Billy clenched his fist, ready to land a punch on him.

With impeccable timing, a familiar voice echoed down the corridor to stall the action.

"Did someone call?"

The new arrival kept us waiting as he tried to force the front door to close properly. "Kitty, why didn't you tell me this was broken? I'd have sent a man up to fix it for you."

"Stuart!" Angelica's face lit up, only to fall again as the kitchen door opened.

"Paul!" said the doctor.

The room fell silent as Paul surveyed the faces staring at him like a Greek chorus waiting for the hero to speak. He looked blankly at Angelica, clearly not recognising her, although she was gazing curiously at him, presumably astonished by the strong resemblance between him and his brother.

"I don't mean to be rude," he said to Angelica, "but who are you and what are you doing in my mother's house? And what are the rest of you doing here so early on a Saturday morning?" He closed his eyes. "Oh God, what's Kitty been up to now?"

I stepped forward and put one hand gently on Paul's arm. Although I didn't like him, he deserved to have the dreadful news broken to him humanely.

"Paul, I'm sorry to tell you that something awful has happened to Kitty. I'm afraid your poor sister has been found dead this morning. It seems she's been murdered, struck a fatal blow on the head with a hammer."

As Paul staggered slightly, I put my arm around his shoulders to guide him to a free chair. I knelt down beside him and took his ice-cold hands. With his bluster and bravado gone, my heart went out to him.

"My little sister?" he murmured. "My little sister, killed? I mean, I know she could be a pain in the rear and half the time she was off her trolley, but she was still my little sister."

He looked away into the distance. "I still remember Mother bringing her home from the hospital, with her little hands screwed up like paws, a twitching pink button

200

of a nose, and a tiny mewing cry. That's why we called her Kitty, you know. My brother and I thought she looked like a kitten, and we were just as delighted as if Mum had come home with a pet for us."

He pulled a handkerchief out of his pocket, blew his nose, wiped his eyes and took a deep breath.

"So what happened? Where is Kitty now? And why the hell aren't the police here? Don't tell me none of you have had the wit to dial 999."

"That's the first thing I did, Paul." I looked at my watch. "That was about half an hour ago. What on earth is keeping them?"

"Bloody roadworks," said Paul tersely. "That bridge closure's slowing everything down. My fifteen-minute journey from Slate Green just took me nearly an hour."

I reached out to touch his hand gently. "You'll have the chance to see her when they get here, if you want to. We're keeping the area sealed off for now, so as not to disturb the evidence before the police get here."

Paul shook his head vigorously. "To be honest, I don't think I could bear to see her in that condition." His eyes darted about the room. "How ever will I break it to Mother?" He gazed imploringly at each of us in turn. "But who? Why? How? Was it a burglar? I've been on at Mother for years to let me fit a proper alarm system, but she wouldn't have it. This place is a gift to a housebreaker, hidden from sight by its big garden and high walls."

"And the front door here hasn't closed properly for days." I put my hands over my eyes. Why hadn't I got Billy to fix it?

Billy coughed. "So, Paul, where have you been since you left the pub last night? You were in no fit state to drive home when I left The Bluebird."

Paul rose unsteadily to his feet, his face suffusing with blood. "What? Is that your roundabout way of asking me to give you an alibi? You think it might have been me? Why would I murder my own sister?"

Billy shrank back. "No, not at all. I didn't mean nothing like that."

Paul crumpled into his chair, elbows on the table, his head in his hands.

"Oh my God, it's all got horribly out of control. My intentions were always the best. You have to believe me. Honestly, I never meant it to end like this."

35 Immaterial

I gasped. "Surely you're not confessing?"

Staring at me in astonishment, Paul uttered a hollow laugh. "No, you stupid girl, of course I'm not confessing. What I meant was, I never meant our family to fall apart like this. I was simply trying to act in their best interests. I'd offered Mother and Kitty free luxury accommodation for life if they let me convert the Manor House into a proper care home. They could even have kept their current bedrooms, after I'd given them a proper makeover and added extra facilities to bring them up to par. They don't need to live like this, you know."

He cast a hand about to indicate the down-at-heel décor. Kitty's attempts to tidy it up this last week couldn't disguise the fact that the place was overdue for modernising.

"They're like those recalcitrant old toffs who insist on staying in their stately homes as they crumble about their ears, when a swift deal with the National Trust would solve all their money worries and give them a grace-and-favour residence for life. And Stuart needn't miss out. He could have shares in the care home for an extra income stream. God knows he could do with the money."

"What did the rest of your family think about your proposition?" I asked gently.

"Oh God, there's another thing I've screwed up. To be honest, I have no idea. I hardly seem to see my wife and son these days. All I am to my wife is a source of funds. She's instilled the same values in our boy. He doesn't see why he should take out a student loan like every other young person. He expects me to stump up the lot for him and save him the bother. Yet once he's qualified as a pharmacist, he'll have no problem paying it back."

He paused, as if wondering how much to take us into his confidence.

"Besides, I don't have that kind of money sitting around in cash. It's all tied up in business investments. Half the time I'm operating on loans, speculating to accumulate, until a project is finished." He shrugged. "I told Fenella if she just sold her sports car, which mostly sits idle on our drive, it would cover the whole of his student loan. But no, apparently it's all down to me."

He looked up, as if startled to find us all still listening. "What am I telling all this to you for? This should be strictly a police matter. Where the hell are they? Why aren't they here, getting on the trail of whoever killed my poor sister?"

"Half-sister," corrected the doctor, unnecessarily.

Paul glared at him.

Angelica tried to soothe Paul. "I'm sure we're all just trying to help. And I don't know about the others, but Billy was very fond of Kitty, you know, and Kitty of him. She told me so last night."

She gazed at Billy warmly for a moment, and the old man's mouth fell open.

"Did she? Did she really? My little cousin Kitty?" His eyes filled with tears.

She nodded, gave him a little smile of sympathy, and continued. "Most murders are committed by someone known to the victim, rather than by a passing stranger. Far too often, family feuds or inheritance issues get out of control. For example – and I'm only speaking theoretically here – you, Paul, might have wanted to oust Kitty from your mother's will."

Paul pointed a shaking hand at the doctor. "As Dr Perkins will tell you, that's preposterous, because he witnessed my mother's will. She left the estate divided equally between Stuart, Kitty and me."

"Really?" That was news to me. "Kitty never knew. Or at least she didn't seem to when I spoke to her about it."

Paul shook his head. "No, but that's only because Mother wanted it kept a secret, to keep Kitty on her best behaviour, and to deter any freeloaders of the kind that used to sponge off her at festivals. To be perfectly honest, it suited me that way, because at least I then didn't have to worry about our four surviving half-siblings from her first marriage trying to get round Mother to include them too."

Angelica looked startled. "There are four more of you? Is there a history of multiple births in your family?"

"No, no twins or triplets. But there were ten of us originally. Three have already died. None of the other four have spoken to Mother for at least twenty years. It's tragic. All she ever wanted was a big family, since losing her own mother at a very young age. Now the older four might just as well have never been born, as far as she's concerned. I hope I never get to that stage with my Dominic. He's not a bad lad, really."

Angelica coughed. "So you were all planning to live here as one big, happy family after your mother's demise? I wonder why Stuart never told me this?"

Paul looked ever so slightly smug. "I was the only one that Mother told. As the eldest of the three of us, you know, and the most responsible. I'd always imagined that when the time came, if Stuart and Kitty wanted me to buy out their shares, I would. Either way, we'd benefit equally."

"So in the absence of Kitty, now there'll be a larger share for Stuart," Angelica said quietly.

Paul turned to her. "Why's that any business of yours? Who are you anyway, and what are you doing here? This is strictly a family matter."

I shifted uncomfortably in my seat, feeling like an intruder myself.

Angelica beamed winningly and held out a well-manicured hand for Paul to shake.

"I'm Stuart's wife, silly. And Paul, can I just say what a pleasure it is to meet you at last, even in such tragic circumstances?" She patted her tummy and looked down to speak to her as yet invisible bump. "Baby, say hello to Uncle Paul."

And with that, Paul burst into tears.

36 Cain and Abel

"You poor fool," sobbed Paul. "Is that what he'd have you believe?"

Angelica looked at him as if he was insane.

"I'm sorry for you, whatever your name is, and sorry for my brother too. And God knows, I'm more sorry than I can say for poor little Kitty. Though it's too late now to tell how much I loved her."

"But not for Bunny," I said gently. "And Bunny will need you and Stuart more than ever now. Do you happen to know where Stuart is, Paul?"

Paul shrugged. "At home with his wife, I suppose. Though when I saw him earlier in the week, he told me he was planning to come here to see Kitty this morning."

"Oh no, he hasn't been at home all week," said Angelica.

Paul's brow furrowed in confusion, prompting the doctor to intervene.

"If it would help you, Paul, I could be the one to break the sad news to Bunny, as her trusted physician of several decades' standing. I've had plenty of experience of imparting sad news during the course of my long career. Years ago, when I worked in geriatric care, it was a frequent duty." He hesitated. "Although of course it's always sad to lose a favourite patient."

Paul sat up straighter. "I know where my duty lies. Stuart and I should go together. It's the least poor Mother deserves. And then I'll see about arranging for a live-in carer to look after her on her return home."

"I presume Kitty's departure will accelerate your plans to turn the Manor House into a care home," said the doctor. "Your dear mother cannot be expected to live on her own, especially after that nasty fall."

Paul's tone turned frosty. "That's my business, thank you. I'll discuss it with Mother and Stuart." He pulled his phone from his pocket. "First I must break the news to Stuart, as soon as I can find him."

Angelica forced a smile. "Good luck with that, Paul, I can never get him to answer his mobile."

Paul ignored her. He'd just pressed the speed-dial for his brother when footsteps rang out in the hall. Paul lowered his phone as we all swivelled round to face the door.

"Oh," said Stuart, staring at Paul and then at me. Then "Oh my!" he said when he saw Angelica, and "Not you!" when he clocked the doctor.

Angelica jumped up to fling her arms about Stuart's neck, and kissed him hard on the lips. Holding on to her arms to stop her ravishing him further, Stuart swung round to glare at Dr Perkins.

"Last time I saw you here, I told you not to set foot in this house again. Good God, I thought once you retired, poor Mother and Kitty would be rid of you."

Paul looked aghast. "Why? What's he done?"

It was Paul's turn to be on the receiving end of Stuart's ire. "If you spent as much time looking out for Mother's health as you do for her property, you wouldn't need me to tell you. I discovered the good doctor here had been prescribing the same sedatives that Kitty was hooked on for so long, the ones she had such trouble getting off when she came back to live with Mother."

"What? Did Mother know? Surely she would have stopped Kitty from taking them."

"It was Mother he prescribed them for, putting temptation right in Kitty's way. Of course, the print on prescription packets is so small that Mother couldn't read it. She just trusted Kitty to give her the right dose of the right stuff at the right time. Dr Perkins knew that. And Kitty would have known exactly what they were. I don't know why he wanted to get Kitty back on to them, but I'm sure he did."

With a superior smile, the doctor turned to Angelica. "I'm afraid he's talking nonsense, my dear. He has no medical knowledge. He's just an accountant. Sums, he can do. Prescriptions, I don't think so."

"I know that your appalling treatment of my sister and your disregard for my mother's wishes add up to malpractice," snapped Stuart.

"Nonsense," said the doctor again. "I've been nothing but protective towards Kitty. Why do you think I didn't call the police when she took your Mother walkabout last weekend, dumping her in that wretched open grave? Because I didn't want to get Kitty into trouble. You must have witnessed their rows. I could quite imagine her pulling that stunt in a fit of pique to teach her mother a lesson."

I jumped up from my chair. "That's ridiculous! What about Kitty's agoraphobia? It was all she could do to bring herself to step outside into her own back garden."

The doctor smirked. "Oh, so you're the expert on medical matters now, are you, Sophie? Well, let me tell you something. Kitty didn't have agoraphobia at all. Simply a controlling mother who insisted she stay indoors to stop her getting into any mischief."

I sat down hard.

Stuart shook his fist at the doctor. "How dare you slander my mother and sister! They may have had their ups and downs – who wouldn't, living together in such isolated company and poor health? – but Kitty would never pull such an outlandish and unkind stunt on her own mother!"

"She certainly won't do it again," returned the doctor coolly. "You see, Stuart, I'm afraid there's bad news about your half-sister."

37 Grassed Up

"Don't tell me she's gone back on the festival circuit." Stuart thrust Angelica's lingering arms away. Angelica huffed and returned to her seat.

Paul got up and went over to his brother. "Stuart, listen, mate, I'm really sorry, but you need to prepare yourself for a shock – a terrible shock." He looked up at the doctor, as if conscious that he was showing him how this should be done. Then he put an arm round Stuart's shoulder. "Come on, mate, I need to borrow you outside."

"Avoid the terrace," I called after them. "Please avoid the terrace till the police get here. And shut the door behind you to keep the cats indoors."

Through the kitchen window, I watched their retreating backs as Paul gently led his little brother out into the garden, well away from Kitty's body. The brothers sat together on a rusting wrought iron bench beneath a shady apple tree full of blossom at the far corner of the garden. The odd petal floated down upon them, like a sympathetic tear. It was probably the closest they'd been in years.

In Stuart's absence, Angelica focused her attention on Dr Perkins. "So, doctor, it appears that although you thought Kitty was a potential danger to her mother, you didn't alert the police when you found Bunny after her fall?"

The doctor held up his hands. "As I just told you, I assumed it was a family feud, sadly fuelled by a combination of Bunny's stubbornness and Kitty's mood swings, the after-effect of years of drug abuse. A pitiful case, and dragging the police into it would not have done either Kitty or Bunny any favours."

"Drug abuse?" asked Angelica. "What kind of drugs?"

The doctor narrowed his eyes in condemnation. "Cannabis. Pot. Marijuana. So much more addictive than most people realise. What starts as a bit of harmless fun can often descend into a sad dependency. I'm afraid it seems Kitty never really shook off the habits from her festival days." He looked down at the floor. "No wonder her behaviour was so erratic. Still, I did what I could to help, as any decent family doctor would do."

"No, you didn't," said Angelica quietly. "You've got her all wrong. She was clean and has been for years. She told me so last night."

Billy nodded.

I knew this was untrue, but hoped that Kitty's little indulgence with the hash brownies the other day might have been a one-off blip to celebrate her temporary freedom from a carer's onerous responsibilities. At any rate, it wouldn't help her now to tell anyone about it.

"And why should we believe you, when you'd never set foot in this village before yesterday, and certainly had no prior knowledge of Kitty or her mother. You're not bright enough to realise that Stuart's been leading you a

212

merry dance. You didn't even know that he is already married."

Angelica drew herself up straight. "Yes, I did. But he and his wife had divorced."

"Of which doubtless you were the cause?"

I jumped in intending to defend her. "His gambling habit might have caused the breakdown of his first marriage." Then I wished I'd kept my mouth shut. It was really none of my business.

Fortunately, Angelica didn't seem to mind. She reached out to touch my arm. "Sophie's right. In fact, that's how Stuart and I met."

"What, in some seedy betting shop?" said the doctor.

"Out of the frying pan into the fire," said Billy. "Still, a very pretty fire you are too, girlie."

Angelica pursed her lips. "Actually, I'm not a girlie, I'm a professional addiction counsellor. I've been helping Stuart to conquer his demons for several years now, and we quickly became very close."

The doctor eyed her stomach. "People don't get much closer than that. Is that how you help all your clients?"

She ignored him. "What's more, I happen to know Kitty wasn't growing pot for her own use. It was to relieve her mother's chronic rheumatic pain – and very successfully so."

The doctor turned to me. "Have you seen how much she's growing out the back there in her little glasshouse? Far too much for one old lady's medicinal use."

Angelica sighed. "I don't suppose it can do her any harm now to tell you she'd been selling her surplus to a local buyer."

I could see why she was a professional counsellor, having managed to extract so much information in a single evening from the reticent Kitty.

"How do you know?" asked the doctor.

"She told me about it last night. Mind you, that was only after she asked me if I wanted any myself. I said no, thank you, because I am pregnant." She blushed. "My goodness, to think I came down here to tell Stuart our good news in person, and here I am telling half the village." She patted her stomach for comfort.

"Anyway, Kitty got all excited about me bringing a new baby into the family, telling me how much her mother loves babies, and she invited me to spend the night. I got the impression that she had been very lonely for a long time, and she was enjoying my company so much that I didn't like to refuse. In fact, I was thrilled to have hit it off with Stuart's sister. However, she told me not to come down from my room for breakfast until half past eight, because her regular customer was calling in at eight o'clock to pick up his order. I don't know who it was."

She looked around the room, as if hoping we might help her out.

"No, but I do," I said. "Dr Perkins."

38 A Lot of Bother

"Dr Perkins was the customer she was expecting. I know, because I saw him arrive from my bedroom window, when I opened the curtains, just after my alarm went off at eight o'clock. I saw him walk past Joshua's house and turn in at the Manor House gate."

"So were you her only customer?" asked Angelica. "Or were there more?"

"I shan't dignify that question with an answer," snapped the doctor, turning away in a huff like a sulky toddler.

I tried not to think about my inadvertent free sample in brownie form. After all, she hadn't offered to sell me any. She was just being sociable. Besides, I had something much more important to say.

"I can think of at least one more. When the Cats Prevention lady, Mrs Petunia Lot, was found unconscious the other day, the doctor drove her home in her car. Hector picked up the bag that she'd left behind and brought it back to the shop. It contained a bag of dried marijuana leaves."

"Marijuana leaves?" echoed Angelica. "Are you sure that's what they were?"

"To be honest, I mistook them for catnip, till Hector put me straight."

The doctor rolled his eyes at my ignorance.

"And what did Hector do with them?" asked Angelica.

"Smoked them, no doubt," sneered the doctor. We ignored him.

"He put them in the shop's safe and was going to give them to Bob when he came home from work. Bob's the nearest thing we've got to a village bobby. He works in the police station at Slate Green, but lives a few doors up from Hector's House."

"So was Mrs Lot a friend of Kitty's?" asked Angelica.

"Oh no, Kitty couldn't stand her," I said. "The woman was always tapping Bunny for donations and dumping stray cats on her."

"Yes, I'd noticed all the cats," said Angelica. "Sweet, aren't they? I'd love a cat."

Right on cue, a fluffy grey cat strode in from the hall and jumped up on her lap, where it curled up and started to purr.

"To be honest," I continued, "I was surprised that Mrs Lot had been to visit Kitty in Bunny's absence, and I was equally surprised that Kitty had let her in. It's obvious now that this wasn't a social call, but a business transaction. I'm guessing the pot was Kitty's only source of personal income besides state benefits."

Angelica sighed. "Stuart told me his sister occasionally slipped him a few quid to help him. I assumed she must have independent means. If he'd known where it came from—" She faltered, her eyes filling with tears.

"Maybe that's how Mrs Lot came to be in no fit state to drive. A bit of over-indulgence with her purchase." I turned to the doctor. "You told Hector it was cough linctus that had knocked her out."

"That's right," said the doctor. "Didn't I show him the empty bottle as evidence? Another sad addict."

"Or else someone made her drink it," said Billy, sitting forward in his chair.

"Surely you don't mean me?" asked the doctor. "Why on earth would I do such a thing? Besides, how could anyone force a person to do that?" He uttered a hollow laugh. "'Excuse me, madam, would you just down this entire bottle of cough linctus?'" He switched to a posh falsetto. "'Oh yes, doctor, anything you say, doctor, right away.' Honestly, if you wanted to knock a person out with a bottle of cough medicine, you'd have a better chance if you just gave them a whack on the head with it."

I cringed at his tactlessness, thinking of how poor Kitty had been killed.

Then I remembered one of the teachers I used to work with always having a bottle of cough mixture in his book bag. I'd caught him swigging out of it more than once, and he'd told me it was just his little helper to get him through a difficult day at work. What could I say? It wasn't illegal.

"Who's to say you didn't have an empty bottle in your possession that you could easily have planted on her?" I said. "Goodness knows what you've got tucked away in that black bag of yours. And why do you still even carry it about with you if you're retired? Does anyone else find that a bit odd?"

We all stared at Dr Perkins black bag which now stood on the kitchen table. He immediately seized it and put it on the floor by his feet, out of our reach.

"Maybe you were taking cough mixture yourself, Doctor, for the codeine?" I continued. "A little self-medication to help you with the strains of your responsible job? I've heard that sometimes doctors, vets and dentists dose themselves up from their pharmacy stocks to get them through the day. That would account for your having an empty bottle to hand."

The doctor spluttered in exasperation. "Good God, what is it with you lot and cough medicine? You're obsessed."

When I nodded in agreement, he looked relieved but as I continued speaking, his face went taut.

"Now that I think about it, I don't believe either cough mixture or pot knocked Mrs Lot out. It was something else. Dr Perkins, I think you slipped her a different drug that you happened to have in your black bag. When Mrs Lot arrived at the Manor House that morning, letting herself in through the unlockable door, as everybody else in the village seems to do these days, she caught you red-handed, buying a supply of marijuana from Kitty."

To my surprise, everyone let me continue unchecked, including the doctor. "So you surreptitiously administered a substance to knock her out and make her forget that she'd seen you, and then let her leave before you did. You also planted a sachet of marijuana leaves and an empty cough mixture bottle in her bag to put everyone off the scent."

"Date rape," said Angelica suddenly. "What's that date rape drug that makes you forget what happened?"

"I've forgotten," said Billy, deadpan.

A vein in the doctor's forehead was starting to throb alarmingly. "So now you're accusing me of being a rapist? My dear girl, have you forgotten? My role is to save

218

people's lives, not to take them away." He gazed beseechingly at Billy as the only other man in the room. "Really, Billy, why are we listening to this senseless drivel? These women are clearly deranged by their hysteria. It'll be the after-effects of the shock."

The more misogynistic he became, the more my rage and confidence grew, like the companion plants flourishing in my aunt's garden.

"Yes, that makes perfect sense," I said. "Some kind of date-rape drug would make her forget seeing you there, so your own marijuana habit would remain a secret between you and Kitty."

The doctor folded his arms tightly across his chest.

"What nonsense you talk, Sophie. As if I could drug a woman against her will right here in front of Kitty!"

Then I remembered. Unlike Kitty, she hadn't passed out in the kitchen. Billy had found her slumped in her car.

"No, of course you didn't. You escorted her to her car, and jabbed something into her there, out of Kitty's sight."

I imagined the doctor leaning over her, all smarmy as he saw her into her car, feigning old-fashioned manners for which I was sure Mrs Lot would be a pushover. I imagined him pulling a loaded syringe from the black bag that he still carried everywhere and plunging it into her arm as she reached for her seat belt. Her arms are so plump she might not even have felt the pinprick.

"That's how come you were so conveniently to hand when Hector came to her rescue. You weren't there by chance. You weren't passing by in the street. You were loitering nearby, to check that the injection took effect."

39 House Call

The doctor tutted as if dismissing an idiot child, but I drew courage from how much his hands were trembling.

"You let her remain in her car, knowing that even when she came round, she'd be incapable of driving properly. Not only did you put her life in danger, but also those of pedestrians and other drivers."

We all glowered at the doctor in horror. He cleared his throat as he raised his hands in denial.

"Oh please, this is just all too foolish for words. I'm sure if you ask Mrs Lot she'll agree that nothing of the sort happened."

"Well, she would say that, wouldn't she?" said Billy. "That's why you drugged her so she'd forget what she saw."

The doctor ignored her. "Here, I'll even give you her phone number. I've got her on my contacts list."

He fumbled in his pocket for his phone.

"Now there's a surprise," said Angelica.

"Except whatever you gave didn't make her forget. Instead, it gave her the idea of alerting the council that this place wasn't fit for Bunny's return. Perhaps her suspicions of drug dealing made them put their visit at the top of their list, which explains why the health inspectors came so quickly after she'd suggested it. Maybe they weren't health inspectors at all, but plain-clothes police officers. Certainly the van they arrived in was unmarked. Hector and I saw it and we spoke to them.

"You're talking rot, Sophie, just trying to distract attention from your own role in this sordid affair."

"What?" I couldn't believe his nerve.

"Yes, Sophie Sayers, I notice you were among the first on the scene in both cases," said the doctor quickly. "At Bunny's accident and at Kitty's death."

My heart skipped a beat. "And so were you, as it happens. Except my role was as innocent bystander, whereas you were totally hands on."

"As a medical professional."

I leaned forward, surer of my ground now. "A retired medical professional, trying a little too hard to hang on to his authority. 'Othello, with his occupation gone', Hector called you."

"Ha! Hector and his highbrow references," sneered Dr Perkins. "Talking of which, hadn't you better get back to his little shop? I'd hate to see Wendlebury missing out on its morning coffee." He turned to Angelica, waving his hand at me dismissively. "She's only a waitress, you know. She knows nothing. The only reason she's been able to solve the odd little mystery in the village in the past is because Hector was behind her, pulling her strings and tipping her off."

That did it.

"No, I'm not. I'm a trained teacher, and a Sunday School teacher too. I'm every bit as much a professional as you are. Or were, at least. So kindly stop giving yourself airs and graces as if you're better than the rest of us."

"Hear, hear," said Billy, bolt upright now.

"Yes, stop it right now," said Angelica.

The doctor gave his biggest sigh yet. "I'm not really retired, you silly girl. I'm just resting. Once a doctor, always a doctor. Because as soon as Paul's turned this place into a care home, and not a moment before time, I shall be taking up the post of resident doctor. We agreed it in principle a long time ago, didn't we, Paul?"

He looked around for confirmation, forgetting Paul had gone out to the garden with Stuart.

"As it happens, I'm looking forward to reviving my particular skills with the elderly. It will mean living on site, of course, or at least in the complex that he has planned. He mentioned he was thinking of buying me your aunt's cottage, Sophie, and he plans to live in Joshua's. Has he made you an offer yet? Wouldn't that be amusing, if I ended up living in your house?"

I flushed but refused to rise to the bait.

"Still, I'm sure you'd cope. As far as I can see, you spend most nights shacked up with Hector above the bookshop, and doubtless he'd welcome an injection of cash from your house sale into his pathetic little business. That's probably what he sees in you. After all, May Sayers did fund his start-up costs when he opened the bookshop a few years ago. You do realise that's why he latched on to you so quickly when you moved into the village, don't you? I saw the pound signs in his eyes, even if you didn't. He's probably thinking he won't even have to pay you a wage once you move in with him."

"Right, that's it." I grabbed a jug of water from the draining board and threw it straight at his contorted face.

He gritted his teeth in a fixed smile, as if it might give him the moral high ground.

Angelica got to her feet and leaned forward, her hands on the table. "I've met a lot of medics in my career, and I have to say you have the worst communication skills I've ever come across. You're nothing but a bully. How dare you talk to Sophie like that, when all she's done is help Stuart's mother and sister? Now you're trying to bludgeon her into submission. Is that how you treat all your patients?"

The doctor clenched his fists. "Bludgeoning? Whatever do you mean? Doctors don't bludgeon."

I paled, picturing the hammer in his hand.

"No," I said slowly. "Doctors operate with precision. Which is how you were able to kill poor Kitty with a single blow to the head. With surgical precision indeed."

Dr Perkins slumped down into a chair as suddenly as if I'd given him a hard slap. "I'm not the only medic in the village. What on earth makes you think it was me?"

But I was on a roll now, incensed by the picture that was forming in my head, thanks to Angelica's prompt.

"Oh, it's all falling neatly into place now. I don't actually believe you meant to kill Bunny. Poor Bunny, she trusted you, and when you visited her first thing early last Saturday morning, she never suspected that you were about to drug her, just as you did Petunia Lot. When you trundled Bunny up to the churchyard in her wheelchair in fancy dress and dumped her there, before the rest of the village was awake, you thought she wouldn't remember seeing you. But she did."

Beads of sweat began to break out on his forehead.

"When Hector and I questioned Bunny about who had visited her that morning, and she said you had, we assumed she was confused, thinking of you at the graveside after her fall. But that was the second time she had seen you that day. The only other witness to the first visit was Kitty. When you let yourself in at the front door, she was already up, having an early morning cup of tea."

The doctor's body was rigid, as if he was trying to prevent himself from showing any reactions.

"I assume you slipped a strong sedative into Kitty's tea as she sat at the kitchen table. That would be easy enough to do. I've seen her put washing up liquid in her tea before now without noticing it. With her out for the count, you'd be free to dope Bunny and wheel her away unhindered. It was early enough on a Saturday morning for you to assume no-one else would be up and about on the High Street to catch you in the act – but if, say, a dog-walker or the milkman happened to notice you, what could look more innocent than a newly retired doctor giving back to his community by taking a lonely old lady out for a stroll? And what could be more natural than her to be dozing contentedly?"

The others nodded in agreement.

"Kitty was still out for the count when Billy went to fetch her as you tended to Bunny in the grave, as you knew she would be. But I don't think you really wanted to kill Bunny. You just wanted to implicate Kitty as an incompetent carer, and so force Paul's hand to turn the Manor House into a care home sooner rather than later, so that you could get your dream job. For goodness' sake, why couldn't you just retire and take up golf or something?"

The doctor shuddered.

"You wanted people to suspect Billy's motives, too, stuffing those empty sleeping pill packets into the pockets of his gardening jacket, as if he'd been the one to sedate them both, if anyone became suspicious afterwards. I bet it was you who then tipped off the police with that ridiculous report of Billy breaking and entering her house, so they'd search his pockets and find the empty drug pockets. It's all falling into place now."

Everyone but the doctor nodded.

"But how on earth would anyone persuade an old lady to down a whole packet of sleeping pills in one go, especially Billy? Bunny may be frail, but her mind is razor sharp."

Billy wiped his face with a grubby handkerchief, clearly relieved to find himself so vindicated.

When the doctor did not respond, I thought I'd made a hideous mistake. For publicly slandering a respected pillar of the local community, I'd probably have to pack my bags and leave the village forthwith. With his self-righteous attitude, he'd be after me with a lawsuit.

When a loud cough came from the direction of the utility room, it became clear that Paul and Stuart had been listening to all the doctor had to say, just out of sight behind the door. Now they came to stand in the doorway, Paul's hand on Stuart's shoulder for support.

"Perkins, if your conscience is clear, you'll have nothing to worry about," said Paul slowly. "The police will check the hammer for evidence. If your DNA's not on it, you are off the hook."

When Dr Perkins pulled a handkerchief from his trouser pocket to mop his brow, a tell-tale pair of plastic surgical gloves came out with it. Before the doctor could bend down to pick them up, I leapt across to stamp on them with my foot and pin them to the floor. He stepped back, startled.

"That's one way to avoid leaving fingerprints," said Paul. He went across to the dresser drawer, pulled out a roll of clear plastic sandwich bags, and put one over each hand like gloves. He bent down to use them to pick up the surgical gloves, which he enveloped in a third bag, knotting the top before slipping it into his own pocket.

"Alternatively, the police might find traces of the hammer's rubber handle on your gloves, doctor."

The doctor shivered, although the room was warm. He looked at each of us in turn. "Surely you don't believe the ridiculous product of this stupid girl's over-active imagination? She clearly spends far too much time reading novels."

"The whole thing does sound ridiculous, I admit," I replied. "But that doesn't mean it didn't happen. After all, this is Wendlebury Barrow."

40 Banged to Rights

The doctor turned pleading eyes on Paul.

"Surely this whole charade just reinforces your conviction that the sooner you turn this into a proper care home, the better?" His tone was wheedling. "Especially now your poor mother won't have Kitty to care for her. It's time to get the professionals in, rather than put her at the mercy of these meddling neighbours. The police will obviously know better and will immediately pursue whoever was the last possessor of the hammer."

When Paul nodded thoughtfully, the doctor must have thought he had won.

"I'm available now, you know," he said. "I can come and start work for you as soon as you like."

I put my hand to my mouth in shock. There was one detail I'd forgotten. "It was a Brady Homes hammer," I said slowly. "Billy said it had the Brady Homes logo on it."

"What?" said Paul. "How did that get there?"

The doctor avoided Paul's stare, slumping down in his seat as if trying to make himself inconspicuous.

229

Billy put his hand up. "It's a fair cop. I borrowed the hammer from The Bluebird last night, and it's something I shall regret for the rest of my days. I was going to return it, honest, just as soon as I'd fixed that dodgy front door. I left it lying on the kitchen table when I came in to remind me to do it this morning. Your men wouldn't even have missed the hammer, Paul, as I was going to put it back by Monday morning." He held out his wrists. "When they finally get here, the coppers can arrest me if they like, but I confess, what with Paul throwing his money about at the bar last night, I didn't think he'd go bust for the loss of a hammer."

I patted Billy on the shoulder to reassure him. "Don't worry, Billy, no-one's going to arrest you. But I think there's now no shadow of a doubt as to the identity of the real murderer."

I turned to the doctor.

"So that's why you instructed us not to call the police when we found Bunny in the grave, and Mrs Lot passed out in her car. You were worried they might realise what you were up to. And you almost got away with it, because we trusted you as our local GP – a true professional – when all you cared about was yourself and your own foolish ego."

The doctor whimpered like an injured dog.

"And why on earth did you dress Mother up in those ridiculous clothes?" asked Paul, running his fingers through his hair. "That fur coat and those bunny ears?"

"To implicate Stuart," I said. "Bunny had recently given Stuart her old fur coat. Kitty told me she thought he'd sell it and keep the money, as he was always short of cash."

"Well, Kitty was wrong," said Stuart. "I gave it to my wife as a peace offering after our last big bust-up, once I'd got it dry-cleaned, of course."

I swept on.

"The doctor knew Stuart had spotted his attempt to derail Kitty with the sedatives she'd been addicted to before and would therefore never have stood for his involvement in the care home. So he tried to frame Stuart as Bunny's assailant to make him fall from grace with her. He knew Bunny had been easily alienated from her other children. With Stuart and Kitty out of the picture, that would clear the way for Paul's plan for the care home – and, critically, for his new job as resident doctor."

"But you never gave me a fur coat," piped up Angelica, with a puzzled frown. "Nor bunny ears. And we've never had a big bust-up."

"Oh, sweetheart," said Stuart, going to stand behind her and gently massaging her shoulders. "I took the fur coat into the dry cleaner's a few weeks ago. When I went back to collect it, the assistant made a grovelling apology. She said they'd had a work experience girl on the counter that week, and when someone giving my name told her they'd lost the ticket, she let him have it, as he was happy to pay the bill." He turned to Dr Perkins. "I don't think you need me to tell you who that customer was, do you, doctor? I remember now, you were behind me in the queue when I dropped it off, which is how you knew it was there. And that's what gave you the idea of blaming me for Mother's abduction. You didn't just want to suggest Kitty was an unfit carer. You wanted to alienate Paul and Bunny from us both."

The doctor turned to me and sneered. "Oh, Sophie, didn't you notice the dry-cleaning label with Stuart's name on it, pinned to the sleeve of the coat for the world to see? Not such a great sleuth after all, are you? I feel you've rather let me down, failing to detect the most obvious clue."

"Well, it didn't take me long to trace where you got the bunny ears from." My voice rose in anger as I remembered Jemima's sorrow at her loss. "How on earth could you implicate an innocent little girl, you brute?"

The doctor looked surprised. "You mean the child who left her ears lying about so carelessly? Oh, they were just a bit of fun. I found them on the pavement on my way to the churchyard and popped them on Bunny's head. I neither knew nor cared who had dropped them. The connection with her nickname made me smile."

He was the only one smiling now.

Angelica shook her head. "I don't get it. Why, when you have all the skills and knowledge of a medical professional at your fingertips, would you go to so much trouble to set up such a contrived and unlikely assault?"

The doctor glared at her as if she were the stupid one. "Because a medical professional would be the last person one would suspect of such a frivolous attack. And it was the sort of thing that a lunatic like Kitty might do, in league with Stuart. He's so easily led." He let out a snort of laughter. "I'm no fool."

And with that remark, the last piece of the jigsaw fell into place for me.

"Whereas a hammer inflicting just the right wound to kill a person at a single blow is the mark of a rank amateur? I suggest when your warped plan to oust Bunny, Kitty and Stuart from the Manor House didn't work, you fell back on a more surgical solution. I'd say you've made rather a hash of it."

"Well," said the doctor, taken aback, "it was my first time."

Angelica put her hands to her temples. "Is everybody in this village insane? What sort of family have I married into? No wonder you didn't want me to meet them, Stuart."

"Ah," said Stuart, "that reminds me. There's something I need to tell you, darling."

41 Saved by the Bell

Just then a buzzing in the pocket of my jeans told me Hector was after me. I pulled my mobile out, pressed "Accept" and held it to my ear, making my way into the hall for some privacy.

"Sophie, where are you? It's nearly ten o'clock. Are you OK?" He sounded anxious rather than angry at my being so late for work. "You're not cross with me about last night, are you?" To be honest, I'd barely given him a minute's thought this morning. "Are you on your way? It's getting pretty busy in here already, and I could do with an extra pair of hands."

"I'm afraid I'm a bit tied up just now."

Hector's voice turned shrill. "Not literally?"

"No, of course not, silly. I'll explain later."

A queue at Hector's trade counter didn't register on my disaster scale right now. He'd have to deal with that issue himself.

"Listen, Hector, just give Becky a ring and see if she's free to cover for me today. You seem to have been doing that a lot lately."

He was silent for a moment. "Yes, OK. But do come and see me, please, as soon as you can. I really need to talk to you about Becky."

We were on our third cup of coffee in the stockroom by the time I'd brought Hector up to date with the sad story of Kitty's dreadful murder, while Becky took care of customers in the shop.

"Now, let me tell you something about Becky," he said, as soon as I'd finished.

I froze. Couldn't he see I'd had more than enough trauma for one day?

"You see, the only reason I've been getting Becky in to the shop is to train her up to cover for you when you're away in Ithaca next month, on that writing retreat you won last summer."

"Is that your only reason?" I asked in a small voice. "She's on your speed dial and everything."

"Becky's fine in an emergency, but she's nowhere near as efficient as you. That funeral book, for example. She took the order down wrong. It wasn't for the Carters, but the Harpers. You know, the family of Neil Harper, whose grave Bunny was dumped in?"

"My goodness, how awful! And the book's still at the Manor House. We'd better get it back before Bunny is discharged. It would be terribly upsetting for her to find it now, especially after what's happened to poor Kitty." I felt my eyes well up. It hadn't yet sunk in that Kitty was really and truly dead. "Besides, it's not as if she needs advice on funeral planning after burying three husbands. Do you want me to pop back up there now? I can let myself in. Billy still hasn't fixed the front door. If the police will let me, that is."

236

Thankfully, the police had arrived a few minutes after the doctor's capitulation. Apologising for their delay due to the bridge closure, they were astonished to find that during that time we'd solved the murder and got the culprit to confess. It was a relief to be allowed to leave once they'd taken my statement.

"We must definitely fix it before Bunny returns, but no need to do it straight away. Besides, we probably won't be allowed anywhere near the Manor House until the police have finished their business there. Anyway, it's too late to help the Harpers now. Neil's daughter phoned this morning, cross that we hadn't delivered the book to her within a couple of days of the order, as Becky had promised. She said she'd got fed up with waiting and bought a copy online, which had come in the next day's post. She expected better from her local bookshop, and I had to agree."

I covered my face with my hands, partly in sympathy at the shaming of Hector's House, and partly to conceal my smile at Becky's fallibility. Perhaps she wasn't competition after all, at least not in terms of employment.

"I'm kicking myself now," Hector continued. "I should have spotted that she'd written the Harpers' phone number in the order book instead of the Carters'. It's just one digit different. I hope we haven't lost their custom for ever." He paused, looking sheepish. "But I confess, I did have another ulterior motive for giving Becky the odd day's work in the shop."

My heart sank, but rose again at his subsequent explanation.

"I thought Carol and Ted could do with some time without her." Ted, a baker from Slate Green, had been dating Becky's mother Carol since Valentine's Day. It was Carol's first romance in decades. "Their relationship is still so new, and while it's lovely that Ted has taken to Becky so well, it's Carol he wants to court, not Becky."

"A bit like you wanting to shut Blossom out of my bedroom when you stay the night with me?"

He grinned. "Yes, I suppose so. Not that I don't like Blossom, any more than Ted dislikes Becky. But Carol's the one he loves and needs to have quality time alone with." I felt a little glow at the parallel. "It will also give Becky a bit of independence. After all, she's too young to get stuck serving behind the village shop counter at her age. It's not easy being a young woman in a village."

"She's about the same age as me," I protested. But with his eye on the time, as ever, Hector wasn't listening. He pulled out his Battersby file from under the counter, and I realised he was expecting yet another visit from their rep. At least this time he hadn't contrived to get me out of the way, but I wasn't sure I wanted to meet her. She might be more alluring than I feared. Perhaps worrying about Becky had distracted me from a greater rival for Hector's affections.

I scuttled behind the tearoom counter as in through the front door tottered an elderly lady. Her long bleach-blonde hair was folded into an elegant French pleat, her elaborate make-up immaculate and her black column dress expensive. She could have been Joanna Lumley's mother. In a tartan trolley in front of her, she was pushing a large pile of Battersby's trademark photographic hardbacks, worth at least £500 at list price.

Hector rushed round from behind the trade counter to greet her. "Mrs Battersby, come in! How lovely to see you again." He held out his arms in welcome, but his eyes were on her books.

"Ahoy there, young Hector! I've brought you more from our returns stock, as promised, and every one in tip-top order, good enough for resale." As she parked her trolley against the trade counter, her many bracelets jangled. "And you know, my son still isn't on to our secret arrangement."

I dropped a cup. As it smashed on the floor, she turned to look at me.

"Hello, my dear, you must be Sophie. Hector's told me all about you."

She teetered over in her high-heeled court shoes to shake my hand.

"I'm Dolores Battersby, of Battersby Books, near Moreton-in-Marsh. My late husband was the founder. Now my son runs it, but I can't stay away. I feel closer to my husband at the print works than I do at home. Besides, an old woman needs a hobby, and mine is recycling good quality returned stock, before my boy can whisk it away into his horrible pulping machine."

Until I started working for Hector, I hadn't realised that booksellers enjoy a sale-or-return ordering system with publishers. Many of them pulp their returns, on the basis that they're not fit for resale once they've been shipped to and from a shop.

"My husband seldom resorted to pulping, but my son insists it protects the brand. But I sneak out the best books while he's not looking and distribute them free of charge to a handful of little local bookshops who deserve a boost. My son has no idea. Ha ha, what larks! He thinks I'm shopping in Cheltenham today. There's no end to how many shopping trips he believes I do!"

Hector glanced across at me, looking slightly guilty that I'd rumbled their little secret. "Tea for two, please, Sophie, and it's on the house."

"Oh, aren't you joining us, Hector?" said Mrs Battersby, making herself comfortable at the tea table nearest me.

I bit back a smile at her misinterpretation. "Yes, do join us, Hector. Feel free."

Hector grinned. "OK, make it three. Right after I've got Mrs Battersby's thank-you present from the stockroom. One bottle or two this time, Mrs B?"

She turned coy. "Oh, just the one, thank you, dear. Must keep my vices under control."

42 Bunny's Easter

"We'll go over the Easter story again after the procession," said Kate, gathering up the sheets of paper on which our Sunday School pupils had been trying to make as many words as possible out of the word donkey. That's not as easy as it sounds. She led us out of the church hall to the car park in which Janet, the village donkey, was waiting patiently on a short rein. Beside her, Billy was almost hidden behind a big basket of palm leaves. The children knew the routine better than I did, rushing up to seize a frond each. Then they stood back and waved them at arm's length with as much wonder and delight as if they were sparklers.

Kate and I herded the children into a crocodile (a line, I mean, not the reptile) behind the donkey. When the line was as neat as it was likely to get under such exciting circumstances, the vicar pulled from his pocket a silver pitch pipe to sound a starting note for our well-rehearsed Palm Sunday hymns. With Kate at the front of the line to take the children in the right direction, and me at the rear to make sure we didn't lose any stragglers along the way, we paraded down the High Street, the children singing at the tops of their voices.

I allowed my gaze to pass beyond Janet to a walking party coming towards us. To my surprise, Becky was pushing the small figure of Bunny in a wheelchair. Beside her walked a young man I'd not seen before, not much more than a teenager, talking animatedly to the old lady, who was nursing little Arthur on her lap. As they came closer, I noticed there was something familiar about the young man's face.

I broke ranks from the crocodile to greet them.

"Hello, Bunny, hello, Becky, hello, Arthur." Cooing, Arthur waved his chubby hand at me. "And I take it you must be Dominic Brady?"

When the boy looked puzzled, Bunny answered on his behalf.

"Yes. Look who's come to see me now, Sophie! My youngest grandson, Paul and Fenella's boy."

Bunny had aged dreadfully since I last saw her. She looked bewildered and lost, like a baby bird fallen from its nest. As a child clutches at a teddy bear for comfort, she clung to Arthur, who sat as solid as a doorstop on her lap, sucking as many fingers as he could fit in his mouth.

"Look, I've got two new friends, too. Your friend Becky is going to look after me till Paul's converted the Manor House, and then she's going to come and work at the care home and have her own flat there. Which means she'll be bringing this little beauty with her."

"You'll have such fun teaching him to explore your garden, won't you, Bunny?" said Becky in a voice loud enough for a deaf old lady to hear. Resting one hand gently on Bunny's shoulder, Becky smiled at me. "Hi, Sophie. It's all true. But tell Hector not to worry. I can still help him at the shop while you're in Greece. Angelica is going to be moving down here soon, and she's going to lead the activities at the care home once it's up and running properly. In the meantime, she can cover for me with Bunny, so I can cover for you."

"I'm just going over the road a minute," said Dominic, spotting his dad standing in the doorway of The Bluebird, beckoning him across.

Bunny fell silent, transfixed by the Sunday School children's joyful singing.

"So is Angelica really Stuart's wife?" I said in too low a voice for Bunny to catch. "Are they really married, or is he a bigamist?"

Becky grinned. "Fortunately neither. Apparently he and his first wife had been planning to divorce for ages and were just waiting to sell their house, but Stuart was so scared of losing Angelica that he pretended it had already gone through. He was trying to split his time between both of their homes, pretending he was away on business. He thought if his first wife suspected there was someone else, he'd get a smaller share in their divorce settlement.

"Angelica had guessed the truth. She's not daft. But she loved him too much to let on. She tried to get him to tell her. She even persuaded him to marry her in some weird ceremony on a beach somewhere, thinking that might push him over the edge, but it didn't. Fortunately it wasn't legally binding, and she knew it – which is just as well for him, or he'd have been prosecuted for bigamy.

"Turns out the equity in his house was so small it didn't make much odds anyway. And his wife had been carrying on with some guy at her office for years, and there were no children involved, so no harm done."

"I'm glad Stuart came out of it all right. He's obviously got his own demons, but he and Angelica clearly adore each other. And they're moving down from the Midlands to live and work at the Manor House."

Becky raised her eyebrows. "I guess that's one gamble that paid off for him, eh? So yes, it's happy families all round." She nodded towards Dominic, who had crossed the road while we were talking to chat to his father. Paul was standing outside the pub, a pint in his hand. "His mum, Fenella, is coming to work there too. Turns out she'd been out of her head with boredom at home, and lonely too, since Dominic went away to university. Paul was so bound up in his business he never realised. Before she gave up work to have Dominic, she used to be an occupational therapist, so care home work will be right up her street."

"A bored occupational therapist?" I raised my eyebrows. "That doesn't bode well."

Becky laughed. "I'm sure she'll be fine. I think this whole business has shaken them all up and reminded them to make the best of what they've got."

She looked away for a moment.

"Oh, Becky," I said gently, realising she must be thinking about her own father, whom she had never known.

She gave me a damp-eyed smile, before reaching out to dust a clump of Blossom's fur off my lapel.

"That reminds me, what's happened to Bunny's cats?" I asked. "Surely Paul's not planning to keep them all in his new care home?"

Becky shook her head. "We're keeping Bunny's favourite, a placid old thing, for its therapeutic value. I've found good homes for the rest. Even Billy's taken two, heaven help them."

I remembered the little beds Billy had made up for the cats at the Manor House.

"Don't worry, they'll be fine. He's a softie underneath."

When the children stopped singing, Bunny reached up to pat Becky's hand, which was still on her shoulder. "So are we going to stand here all day?" she cried. "I think little Arthur wants his dinner."

Becky laughed. "You mean you do, Mrs Carter!" I was glad to see Bunny smile at last.

I bent down to kiss Bunny's sunken cheek, and as I did so she took my hands in hers and gave them a feeble squeeze. I was glad that Kitty's death had glued the rest of her fractured family together, though it was heartbreaking that it took a murder to resolve their feud. I wondered whether she might yet make peace with the remaining children from her first marriage. I sincerely hoped so.

Then Kate gave me a shout to rejoin the crocodile as it did a U-turn to pass back up the High Street to the church. The children dished out palm crosses from Janet's panniers to villagers who came out to wave at our little procession as we passed by. Some brought carrots and apples for the donkey and sneaked sweets to the children, even though it was still Lent.

As we passed the churchyard, just prior to turning in at the gate for the Palm Sunday service, I couldn't help but notice the fresh soil covering Kitty's grave, marked by a small wooden cross. In the future, I planned to take a few flowers to her every time I visited Auntie May's grave. But not too many, and not for too long. Life is meant to be lived, and I had plenty to look forward to, not least my writing break in Ithaca, far away from Wendlebury Barrow and its endless surprises. If this latest case had taught me anything, it was to seize the day, because, like Kitty Carter, one never knew which day would be one's last.

As I followed the singing children up the path and through the church porch, it was not their voices, but Billy's that was reverberating in my head:

"The grave's a fine and private place
But none, I think, do there embrace."

Not even Bunny Carter.

*If you enjoyed reading this book,
you might like to spread the word to other readers
by leaving a brief review online —
or just tell your friends!
Thank you.*

Like to know when
Debbie Young's next book
is ready for you to read?
Sign up for her free Readers' Club
and download a free ebook,
The Pride of Peacocks,
set in Wendlebury Barrow and
featuring Sophie and friends at:
www.authordebbieyoung.com

Acknowledgements

Enormous thanks to all the people who have helped make this a better book:

- Orna Ross, as ever, for her wise and sensitive mentoring of the creative process (google her Go Creative! Series)
- Novelists Lucienne Boyce, David Penny and Belinda Pollard for their insightful beta reading and tact
- Alison Jack, my editor, always patient, capable, and dependable
- Rachel Lawston of Lawston Design for another wonderful book cover design
- My late English teacher, friend and mentor, Joe Campbell, for introducing me to *To His Coy Mistress* and making me a fan of Andrew Marvell for life
- To my friend Sue Hewer for naming Sophie's kitten Blossom – and fellow author John Lynch for Hector's suggestion of Satan
- To my family for setting the bar for relationships very high

Debbie Young

Also by Debbie Young

Sophie Sayers Village Mysteries
Best Murder in Show (1)
Trick or Murder? (2)
Murder in the Manger (3)
Murder by the Book (4)
Murder Your Darlings (6)
Murder Lost and Found (7) – coming 2021

Staffroom at St Bride's School Mysteries
Secrets at St Bride's (1)
Stranger at St Bride's (2)
Scandal at St Bride's (3) – coming 2021

Tales from Wendlebury Barrow (Quick Reads)
The Natter of Knitters
The Clutch of Eggs

Short Story Collections
Marry in Haste
Quick Change
Stocking Fillers

Essay Collections
All Part of the Charm:
    A Modern Memoir of English Village Life
Young By Name:
    Whimsical Columns from the Tetbury Advertiser

More
Sophie Sayers
Village Mysteries

Best Murder in Show
(Sophie Sayers Village Mysteries #1)

A dead body on a carnival float at the village show.

A clear case of murder in plain sight, thinks new arrival Sophie Sayers - but why do none of the villagers agree? What dark secrets are they hiding to prevent her unmasking the murderer, and who holds the key to the mystery? Can Sophie unearth the clues tucked away in this outwardly idyllic Cotswold village before anyone else comes to harm, not least herself?

For fans of cosy mysteries everywhere, Best Murder in Show will make you laugh out loud at the idiosyncrasies of English country life and rack your brains to discover the murderer before Sophie can.

"A cracking example of cosy crime"
Katie Fforde

Available in paperback and ebook
ISBN 978-1-911223-13-9 (paperback)
ISBN 978-1-911223-14-6 (ebook)

Trick or Murder?
(Sophie Sayers Village Mysteries #2)

Just when Sophie Sayers is starting to feel at home in the Cotswold village of Wendlebury Barrow, a fierce new vicar arrives, quickly offending her and everyone else he meets.

Banning the villagers' Halloween celebrations seems the last straw, even though he instead revives the old English Guy Fawkes' tradition. What dark secret is he hiding about Sophie's boss, the beguiling bookseller Hector Munro? And whose body is that outside the village bookshop? Not to mention the one buried beneath the vicar's bonfire piled high with sinister effigies.

Sophie's second adventure will have you laughing out loud as you try to solve the mystery, in the company of engaging new characters as well as familiar favourites from Best Murder in Show.

"Debbie Young delves into the awkwardness
of human nature in a deft and funny way:
Miss Marple meets Bridget Jones."
Belinda Pollard, Wild Crimes series

Available in paperback and ebook
ISBN 978-1-911223-20-7 (paperback)
ISBN 978-1-911223-19-1 (ebook)

Murder in the Manger
(Sophie Sayers Village Mysteries #3)

When Sophie Sayers's plans for a cosy English country Christmas are interrupted by the arrival of her ex-boyfriend, Damian, her troubles are only just beginning. Before long, the whole village stands accused of murder.

Damian says he's come to direct the village nativity play, but Sophie thinks he's up to no good. What are those noises coming from his van? Who is the stranger lurking in the shadows? And whose baby, abandoned in the manger, disappears in plain sight?

Enjoy the fun of a traditional Christmas festive season with echoes of Charles Dickens' A Christmas Carol *as Sophie seeks a happy ending for her latest village mystery – and her budding romance with charming local bookseller Hector Munro.*

> *"The funniest opening line in a novel, period.*
> *I can't get enough of the*
> *Sophie Sayers Village Mystery series."*
> *Wendy H Jones,*
> *author of DI Shona McKenzie thrillers*

Available in paperback and ebook
ISBN 978-1-911223-22-1 (paperback)
ISBN 978-1-911223-21-4 (ebook)

Murder by the Book
(Sophie Sayers Village Mysteries #4)

Sophie Sayers' plans for a romantic Valentine's night at the village pub didn't include someone being shoved to their death down its ancient well.

But as no-one witnessed the crime, will it ever be solved in this close-knit English village where everyone knows each other - and half of them are also related?

It will be solved if Sophie Sayers has anything to do with it. But can she stop eager teenage sidekick Tommy Crowe unmasking her boyfriend Hector's secret identity in the process, causing chaos to his precarious bookshop business?

A whole shoal of red herrings will keep you guessing as tempers flare and old feuds catch fire in this lively mystery about love, loyalty and family ties, set in the heart of the idyllic English Cotswolds. Idyllic unless you happen to be a murder victim.

"An assured and delicious sequel"
Susan Grossey,
author of the Sam Plank Mysteries

Available in paperback and ebook
ISBN 978-1-911223-26-9 (paperback)
ISBN 978-1-911223-26-7 (ebook)

Murder Your Darlings
(Sophie Sayers Village Mysteries #6)

When Sophie Sayers joins a writers' retreat on a secluded Greek island, she's hoping to find inspiration and perhaps a little adventure. Away from her rural English comfort zone, she also takes stock of her relationship with her boyfriend Hector.

But scarcely has the writing course begun when bestselling romantic novelist Marina Milanese disappears on a solo excursion to an old windmill. First on the scene, Sophie is prime suspect for Marina's murder. When a storm prevents the Greek police from landing on the island to investigate, Sophie must try to solve the crime herself – not easy, when everyone at the retreat has a motive.

As she strives to uncover the truth about Marina's fate, Sophie arrives at a life-changing decision about her own future.

"The change of location works brilliantly and Debbie Young's excellent handling of the story keeps you guessing all the way through."
Juliette Lawson,
author of the Seaton Carew Sagas

Available in paperback and ebook
ISBN 978-1-911223-55-9 (paperback)
ISBN 978-1-911223-56-6 (ebook)

Introducing the Staffroom at St Bride's

(School Stories for Grown-ups)

Secrets at St Bride's
(St Bride's School Stories #1)

When **Gemma Lamb** takes a job at a quirky English girls' boarding school, she believes she's found the perfect escape route from her controlling boyfriend – until she discovers the rest of the staff are hiding sinister secrets.

- Hairnet, the eccentric headmistress
- Oriana Bliss, Head of Maths & master of disguise
- Joscelyn Spryke, the suspiciously rugged Head of PE
- Mavis Brook, selling off the school library books
- Max Security, creepy night watchman

Even McPhee, the school cat, is leading a double life.

Tucked away in the school's beautiful private estate in the Cotswolds, can Gemma stay safe and build a new independent future? With a little help from her new friends, she's going to give it her best shot…

This novel was shortlisted for **The Selfies Award 2020**, *given to the best independently published fiction in the* UK.

"The perfect book - I loved it!
Thank you so much for writing
such an entertaining and intelligent book."
Katie Fforde, Sunday Times bestselling novelist

Available in paperback and ebook
ISBN 978-1-911223-43-6 (paperback)
ISBN 978-1-911223-41-2 (ebook)

Stranger at St Bride's
(St Bride's School Stories #2)

When an American stranger turns up claiming to be the rightful owner of the St Bride's estate, teacher Gemma Lamb fears losing her job, her home, and her hopes for a relationship with charismatic PE teacher Joe Spryke.

When Hairnet, the headmistress, accepts the stranger's claim due to his remarkable resemblance to the school's founder, it's down to Gemma to save the school, with a little help from her friends in the staffroom. That's if inventive pranks by the girls – and the school cat McPhee – don't drive him away first.

This sequel to Secrets at St Bride's, *shortlisted for* **The Selfies Award 2020**, *is full of seasonal fun as the school celebrates the highlights of the autumn term, from Halloween to the Christmas Fair.*

"An absolute delight of an easy, comfortable entertaining read."
Helen Hollick, author of the Jan Christopher Mysteries

Available in paperback and ebook
ISBN 978-1-911223-43-6 (paperback)
ISBN 978-1-911223-41-2 (ebook)

Printed in Great Britain
by Amazon

59218863R00161